D1526684

EARTH 2788

ABOUT THE AUTHOR

Janet Edwards lives in England and writes science fiction. As a child, she read everything she could get her hands on, including a huge amount of science fiction and fantasy. She studied Maths at Oxford, and went on to suffer years of writing unbearably complicated technical documents before deciding to write something that was fun for a change. She has a husband, a son, a lot of books, and an aversion to housework.

Visit Janet online at her website www.janetedwards.com to see the current list of her books. You can also make sure you don't miss future books by signing up to get an email alert when there's a new release.

ALSO BY JANET EDWARDS

Set in the Hive Future

TELEPATH

Set in the Portal Future

The prequel novellas:-

EARTH AND FIRE: An Earth Girl Novella

FRONTIER: An Epsilon Sector Novella

The Earth Girl trilogy:-

EARTH GIRL

EARTH STAR

EARTH FLIGHT

The Earth Girl prequel short story collection:-

EARTH 2788: The Earth Girl Short Stories

Other short stories:-

HERA 2781: A Military Short Story

JANET EDWARDS

EARTH 2788

The Earth Girl Short Stories

.

CONTENTS

INTRODUCTION

For some people, reading these stories will be their first encounter with the future universe of the Earth Girl trilogy, where people use interstellar portals to travel between hundreds of colony worlds scattered across space. Others will have already read at least one of the books in the Earth Girl trilogy, so they'll be meeting some old friends and learning more about them.

The three books in the Earth Girl trilogy were written entirely from the viewpoint of one character. Earth Girl, Earth Star, and Earth Flight are telling Jarra's story: her fight not just for equality, but for self-belief. It's right that the reader should experience that story through Jarra's eyes, but, as the writer, I know as much about the other characters as about Jarra herself. There were many points in the trilogy when I wanted to write more about the varied backgrounds of the other characters but couldn't, either because there wasn't space in the book or because Jarra wouldn't know the private thoughts and secrets of other people.

So the title story of this collection is written from Jarra's viewpoint in the same way as the books, but the rest of the stories are told through different eyes and cover some of the events I couldn't mention in the trilogy. They're all prequel short stories, set in the year 2788 just a few months before the start of the trilogy. Like the pieces in a jigsaw puzzle, whether you read them before or after reading the books shouldn't matter – they should all fit together to add to the picture of the future.

In the year 2788, humanity has settled colony worlds in five sectors of space, is in the process of colonizing a sixth, and has already chosen the sector that will be colonized next. Each sector of space contains about two hundred colony worlds, and has its own distinctive culture that impacts the lives of the people living there. I'd deliberately included characters from as many different sectors as possible in the Earth Girl trilogy. Telling their stories takes the reader on a tour of Earth and the different sectors of space in the year 2788, so I've chosen the titles to reflect that.

I've really enjoyed writing these stories. I hope you enjoy reading them too. If you do, then you can find more information about my books and short fiction at my website: www.janetedwards.com

EARTH 2788 - JARRA

Earth, June 2788.

My best friend, Issette, followed me into the foyer of our Next Step. We'd both lived in Hospital Earth residences since we were babies, first Nursery, then Home, and now Next Step. Every one of those residences had an identical foyer, an echoing empty space with standard, institutional, pale green walls, and a single portal in the centre.

Issette watched me dial the portal. I daren't enter the code for our real destination, because Hospital Earth had systems that monitored the portal travel and credit records of its wards. If the systems spotted that any of my destinations or purchases were flagged as unsuitable, they'd automatically notify the Principal of my Next Step, and she'd drag me into her office for a lecture.

Our destination today wasn't just flagged as unsuitable, but utterly forbidden. That meant the systems wouldn't stop after alerting the Principal. Alarms would start flashing and the police would be after me, so I had to dial the closest respectable destination instead. Earth Europe Transit 3.

As the portal established, I turned to frown at Issette. "You really shouldn't get involved in this," I said, for the third time in the last hour.

Issette grinned at me. "I'm coming with you, Jarra."

3

I groaned. "Well, if we get caught, then you have to put all the blame on me. Tell everyone that I pushed you into doing this."

I stepped through the portal, leaving Next Step behind me. On Year Day 2789, Issette and I would become 18, legally adult, and leave this place forever. There'd be no more Principal lecturing us, no more systems spying on us, no more staff searching our rooms. We'd finally be free. That freedom was still six months, eight days, and thirteen hours away. I wasn't quite at the point of counting the minutes. Yet.

I appeared in the main hall of Europe Transit 3, moved clear of the red floor area that marked the arrival zone, and turned to watch Issette come through the portal behind me. This was just one in a row of over twenty local portals, and a constant stream of people were moving between them and the area that held the special longer distance inter-continental portals to Earth America, Asia, Africa and Australia. Issette and I hurried across to a quiet spot out of the way of the other travellers, and I looked round carefully. I could only see one security guard, but he was uncomfortably close to us.

We went over to the wall and leaned casually against it. Issette checked her lookup and gave a theatrical yawn. I tried to act bored instead of nervous. Anyone looking at us should think we were waiting for a friend who was late. It was pure chance that we were doing our waiting right next to a small white door in the wall. I glanced across at the security guard, willing him to go and stand somewhere further away.

I didn't know why Issette was insisting on coming with me. I was the one with the history of rebellion, not her. I didn't even know why I was doing this myself. I was never any good at making sense of my own emotions. This was somehow like the crazy thing I did back when I was 14. It was about frustration, defiance, and looking my enemy right in the face.

A woman walked up to the security guard. I couldn't hear what she was asking him, but he nodded, took out his lookup, and frowned down at it, clearly checking some information. Issette and I would never get a better chance than this, so I turned to the door beside me, and entered a code into the lock plate.

I held my breath as I waited to see if the code was accepted. I'd had no idea how to get it myself, so I'd nagged my friend Keon for days until he'd agreed to help. Keon was incredibly smart, but also incredibly lazy. If he'd given me a random number to shut me up...

The door was opening! I hurried inside, Issette followed me, and I closed the door behind us. We were in a grey flexiplas corridor now, with the glows on a minimum setting. It seemed very dark compared with the bright lights outside, and further down the corridor was utter blackness. I heard Issette gasp.

"I hadn't realized there wouldn't be proper lighting in here," I said. "We'd better go back."

"No," said Issette. "I'm totally fine. I'm not scared of the dark anymore. My psychologist helped me overcome my fear."

I wasn't convinced. For one thing, I didn't believe the compulsory sessions with a psychologist that Hospital Earth inflicted on its wards had helped me with anything. For another, I could hear Issette's voice shaking.

"We could get torches and come back later," I said.

"Jarra, Jarra, Jarra, stop wasting time," she said. "My eyes are getting used to the darkness now. I told you that I'm totally fine."

"You're more than totally fine, you're totally amaz." I hugged her, then led the way along the corridor past a set of numbered doors that probably hadn't been opened for a century or more. The blackness ahead of us retreated as the ceiling glows detected our movement and automatically turned on. I glanced over my shoulder, and saw the ones behind us going out. The effect was chaos creepy, as if the darkness was a living thing chasing after us, and my mind started conjuring up unwelcome memories of scenes from horror vids.

We reached a junction, took a left turn, and moved on in our own small bubble of light. Some of the glows were flickering strangely now, which could be a sign they were failing from old age. If all the lights went out, how would I stop Issette from panicking while we groped our way through this maze of corridors? We could completely lose our way in the pitch darkness, and then...

I shoved that thought aside, and kept talking in the most cheerful tone I could manage. I wasn't just trying to keep Issette's fear at bay now, but also my own. "I found out about these corridors by pure accident. For the last hundred years, they've only been used as an emergency access route for when a solar storm brings down the Earth portal network. I was reading about what happened back in 2693 when..."

"No!" Issette interrupted me. "This place is dreadful enough without having to listen to one of your boring history lectures as well. Bad, bad, Jarra!"

I laughed and turned right. "Sorry. Careful on this bit, there's quite a steep slope down, but we're nearly there now."

Two minutes later, we were facing a door at the end of the corridor. The locks were to keep people out, not in, so I just had to wave my hand at the door release and it opened. I went through into sudden brightness, tugging Issette after me, before closing the door and looking hastily round. I'd aimed to arrive through this door in particular, because the plans I'd found on the Earth data net had showed a bank of food dispensers in front of it. The dispensers must have been replaced a dozen times since those plans were made, but they were still in the same position, so we were safely hidden behind them.

I leaned my back against the sheltering bulk of one of the machines, turned to Issette, and gave a breathless giggle of jubilation. We'd made it. No one under the age of 18 was allowed through the security checks without a parent or legal guardian, but we'd bypassed them and reached the forbidden territory of Earth Europe Off-world.

Issette giggled back at me. "I'd no idea this place was so close to Europe Transit 3. The portal codes are totally different, so I assumed... What now?"

I had last minute nerves about leaving our hiding place, but we were wearing our best clothes, and Issette had spent nearly an hour adding makeup to our faces in the same style as a famous Alphan vid star. We must look at least 18, if not 20, and surely no one could tell we weren't norms just by looking at us.

"Now we go and look at the information display like genuine interstellar travellers planning our route. Ready?"

Issette gulped, ran her fingers over her frizzy hair to smooth it into place, and nodded. I led the way out from behind the dispensers, and saw a vast open area, even bigger than a Transit. There was a huge array of seating in the centre, where a scattering of people sat facing the...

I'd intended to look adult, sophisticated, and bored as I walked straight across to the information display, but I couldn't help stopping and staring at the portals. Inter-continental passenger portals looked almost identical to local portals, just a fraction thicker, but these were very different. Ten matching interstellar portals, with huge chunky rims. The nearest one was active and locked open, the green sign above it saying "Outgoing Adonis." A short queue of people were waiting their turn to step through. The woman at the head of it held the hand of an excited boy who looked about 5 years old. A uniformed man gave her a nod, she picked up the child, walked into the portal and vanished.

I heard myself make a soft sound of pure longing. The woman and child were on another planet now. Adonis, the closest colony world to Earth. Adonis, the first planet to be colonized back in 2310 at the start of the Exodus century that emptied Earth. Adonis, capital planet of Alpha sector, with its historic Courtyards of Memory and the proud traditions of the Adonis Knights.

There was a tugging at my arm, and I heard Issette's frantic whisper. "Jarra, you can't keep standing here and staring like this. People will notice us and we'll get caught!"

She was right. I was acting like a total nardle. I forced myself to turn my head away from the portals, and walked across to the wall that glowed with portal information and lists of staggering off-world portal costs. Portal 1 was marked in green and locked open for Adonis outgoing traffic. Portal 2 was in red and locked open for Adonis incoming. Portals 3 to 6 had a list of times for the scheduled incoming and outgoing block portal slots to and from assorted Alpha sector worlds, listed in red and green as appropriate. Portals 7 and 8 were amber, flagged for use by anyone who was chaos rich and willing to pay four or five times the cost of a block portal journey for the privilege of dialling an interstellar portal link at their own convenience rather than waiting. Portals 9 and 10 were grey, because...

I hastily turned my head away from the information for portals 9 and 10, and went into the nearest vacant journey planning booth. Issette squeezed in beside me, and gave me a grin.

"Where shall we go?" she asked. "There are a couple of hundred planets in Alpha sector to choose from."

I shook my head. "Why settle for Alpha sector? Let's go all the way to the frontier. We can be colonists going to one of the new planets in Kappa sector." I tapped the Kappa sector option on the booth display and laughed. "Several planets in Kappa sector are trying to improve their low ratio of female to male colonists by offering subsidized travel for incoming female colonists. Do we want subsidized travel?"

"Definitely," said Issette, entering into the spirit of the fantasy. "I couldn't get to Adonis on my credit balance, let alone Kappa sector."

I selected subsidized travel, and a holo of the three concentric spheres of humanity appeared. The first sphere was Alpha sector, with Beta, Gamma and Delta surrounding it to form a larger sphere. Beyond those, all the frontier sectors had been added to complete the third sphere. All of those sectors were marked as uncharted, of course, except for newly colonized Epsilon and Kappa.

This holo was the fancy version, with hundreds of thousands of dots for star systems, the scattered brighter dots showing those which had an inhabited world. A white line zigzagged its way out from Earth at the centre to show our journey to Kappa sector.

"We join a block portal to Alpha Sector Interchange 2 in three hours' time," I said, "then we have four more block portals to get us from there, across Gamma sector, and to Kappa Sector Interchange 1. We should arrive there in thirty-eight hours' time, and a representative of the Kappa Colonization Advisory Service will help us make our final choice of a colony world."

Issette wrinkled her nose in mock disgust. "A thirty-eight hour journey is ridiculous. I thought they were desperate for female colonists."

I giggled. "They aren't desperate enough to pay for them to dial a special cross-sector portal link."

We moved across to the seating area, and chose chairs well away from everyone else. The people sitting in the waiting area looked oddly alike, arms huddled round themselves to avoid touching anything, and wearing matching expressions of pained distaste. Most of them were sitting in total silence, but the couple to my left were arguing.

"I can't believe you made me come here just to save a few credits," said the woman.

"It's not just the credits," said the man. "Avoiding Earth entirely meant an extra thirty-one hours' journey time as well. It's in the centre of Alpha sector, and has five Off-worlds, so a lot of traffic is routed this way."

"Well, it shouldn't be," said the woman. "Nobody wants to come to Earth. It's not safe!"

The man sighed. "We've had this discussion ten times already. It's been scientifically proven there's no medical risk in spending time on Earth."

"The doctors can't know that. They've absolutely no idea what causes the problem. I know there won't be any of *them* in here with us, but..."

She gave a graphic shudder of disgust, and I wondered what she'd think if she knew two of *them* were sitting only a few chairs away from her. I was tempted to go over and tell her what I was. I wanted to see the look of horror on her face and laugh at her, but I couldn't. It wouldn't just be me who got into trouble for sneaking in here, but Issette as well.

The couple lapsed into sulky silence. I tried to forget them, and sat watching the people arriving from other worlds. Issette was studying their clothes, but I was looking at their faces. Most of them were coming over to the waiting area, so Earth was just one step on their journey. I concentrated on the ones heading for the exit, the ones who were actually visiting Earth, wondering what had brought them to such an unpopular destination.

Portal 4 flared into life with a new incoming block portal, and a large group of people in medical uniforms came through. One of Earth's major specialities was medicine, so these were probably off-world students here for part of their training. Behind them walked a couple with two children, both girls.

The older girl was about my age. I pictured the life she had, and thought how it could have been mine too if the genetic dice had landed differently. I could have been growing up with a family on a distant world. I could have been portalling to Earth for a visit. I could have had everything, instead of...

Issette gave me a painful jab with her elbow, and I turned to frown at her. "Ouch!"

"Shhh," she hissed. "Look over there!"

She was pointing towards portal 7. Someone had obviously just arrived through it, because a set of hover bags were still appearing. I watched them chase after their owner and gather up in a group behind him, then looked at the owner himself and gasped. He was young, attractive, and dressed in clinging clothes that showed bare patches of skin in shocking places. I stared at him for a moment, totally grazzed, before turning my head away.

"He must be from one of the planets in Beta sector," said Issette, still happily studying him. "Nowhere else has clothes like that. He's got to be filthy rich to dial interstellar instead of block portalling, so maybe he's from their capital planet, Zeus. He's got nice legs, hasn't he?"

She was using the polite word, "legs," but I could tell from the way she said it that she really meant a far more private area. I frowned at her. "Issette, behave yourself!"

She turned her head for a second to give me a wicked grin, before staring at the man again. "It's not my fault he's dressed like that, and everyone else is looking too."

I gave in to temptation and had another look myself. The man did have extremely nice legs, and you could see an awful lot of them! He was dark-haired, and I generally preferred men with the much rarer blond hair, but in this case I could definitely...

At this point, a security guard hurried up, threw a blanket round the man's shoulders, and had a whispered conversation with him. The man laughed, but nodded, and went off with the blanket wrapped firmly round him.

Issette sighed. "Pity."

After that, we watched a group of young people come through portal 2, chattering to each other in the classic drawling voices of aristocratic Alphans. Judging from the snatches of conversation I could hear, they were pre-history students returning from a break on their home world. I was planning to study pre-history myself, so I listened avidly, trying to work out which of Earth's ruined cities they'd be excavating. Since they'd portalled into Earth Europe Off-world, it was probably London, Paris Coeur or Berlin. Madrid Main Dig Site was still closed for clean up after an ancient storage facility had a major radioactive leak. Rome didn't accept students. Budapest was...

I heard the sound of someone shouting, and twisted round in my seat to look across at where people were entering Earth Europe Off-world the legal way through the security checks. A man clutching a plant was arguing with the guards. I shook my head in disbelief. Did he seriously expect to stroll through an interstellar portal carrying that? The dimmest of nardles should know that introducing random plants or animals to an alien world could cause havoc with the eco system. Even some of the most carefully planned introductions of Earth species to colony worlds had caused unexpected problems.

Apparently this dim nardle truly didn't know that, because he was shouting at the security guards so loudly now that everyone in the waiting area could hear him. "You're a bunch of officious nuking idiots!"

Issette turned to me and pulled a buggy-eyed, shocked face, which could either have been at the man's stupidity or at him using the nuke word in public. I covered my mouth with both hands to stop myself laughing. If I was one of the security guards, I'd be strongly tempted to let the man try to take his precious plant through an interstellar portal. The bio-filters would instantly shut the portal down, and he'd be fined a fortune for attempting to breach interstellar quarantine.

The security guards had a lot more patience than I did, because they just made soothing noises, took the offending plant into custody, and let the aggrieved traveller stalk off through portal 1 to Adonis.

I was still exchanging grins with Issette when portal 7 came to life again. We both turned to see if this was another scantily-clad man from Beta sector, but this time it was a couple in the unremarkable clothes of Gamma sector. The woman was openly crying, uncaring of who might see her, and the man appeared to be torn between comforting her and keeping his distance. I'd worked out what was happening here even before an older woman in the formal grey and white uniform of a Hospital Earth Child Advocate hurried up to meet them.

The man spoke before she could. "There's no throwback genes in my family. This must be a ridiculous mistake, unless..."

He turned to give a suspicious look at the crying woman, and she seemed to forget her tears as she glared at him in outrage. "There's never been any apes in my family. It must be you!"

The advocate hastily intervened. "Please remember that on Earth we prefer to use the official term, Handicapped, rather than derogatory slurs. I'm sorry, but there's no mistake. Your son was born with a flawed immune system, so he can't survive on any world other than Earth."

She paused for a moment. "There's a random one in a thousand risk even with two normal parents, so this can happen to absolutely anyone, but you'll be happy to hear your son was portalled here in time to save his life. He's currently in a Hospital Earth Infant Crash Unit, but his condition should soon be stable enough for you to visit him. Before then, I'd like to give you information on all the options available to help parents move to Earth to be with their Handicapped babies."

The three of them headed off to the exit, with the advocate still talking in bracingly cheerful tones, but I could tell she was wasting her time. The man had a rigid, cold expression on his face, and the woman had the distant look of someone already rehearsing the speech she'd make to explain how she couldn't possibly give up everything and move to Earth to take care of her son. She'd use the same excuses they all did, claiming it was nothing to do with the embarrassment or the damage to her lifestyle, but because she felt it was best to let the child grow up with his own kind.

This couple were going to do what 92 per cent of the parents of Handicapped babies did. They were going to hand their son over to be raised as a ward of Hospital Earth, turn their backs on the reject, and walk away. That was what my parents had done when I was born. That was what Issette's parents had done. That was what the parents of all my friends at Next Step had done.

I turned to look at portals 9 and 10 for the first time. They were dark, but occasionally their lights would blink as they relayed a portal signal for an incoming medical emergency, sending a newborn Handicapped baby directly to a Hospital Earth Infant Crash Unit.

I glanced at Issette's face, saw she was on the verge of tears, and stood up. "We'd better go now."

We walked back to the door hidden behind the food dispensers. I'd just entered the code into the lock plate, and was opening the door, when I heard a sudden shout.

"Hey! Where are you going?"

I looked round, and saw a security guard heading towards us. I grabbed Issette's hand, dragged her through the door with me, and kicked it closed behind us. Hopefully, the guard wouldn't know the code to open the door and...

There was a series of clicks from the lock plate, and I saw the door start opening again. I groaned, turned, and ran down the corridor, tugging Issette along with me. The ceiling glows overhead were automatically turning on for us, just as they'd done earlier, but now we were moving too fast for them. We were running on the edge of darkness, with the pool of light always a pace or two behind us. I could hear the sound of heavy footsteps chasing after us, and noisy, irregular gasps for breath from Issette. Was she breathing like that because of the physical effort of running, or because she was about to panic?

There was a dark shadow on the wall to my left. A side corridor! I turned and skidded into it, towing Issette with me. I was hoping that we could hide while the guard ran past us, but of course the glows overhead started turning on, signalling our location.

"Nuke it!" I cursed my own stupidity and ran on, taking another couple of random turns. We'd been moving faster than the guard to start with, but now I was horribly aware the footsteps behind us were getting steadily closer. Our best chance would be to split up, because a single guard could only chase one of us, but I couldn't leave Issette on her own in the darkness.

I was expecting to be grabbed from behind at any moment, when the sound of footsteps suddenly stopped. I risked turning my head for a second, and saw the guard standing still, leaning against the wall and panting for breath.

"He's given up!" I said.

We ran on down another couple of corridors, before stopping to rest and get our breath back. I was rejoicing in our escape, when Issette spoke in a shaky voice.

"Is it far to the way out?"

There was a sick feeling in my stomach as I tried to remember all the turnings we'd taken during the chase. We must be far away from the route we'd used to get to the Off-world. I tried to keep my voice calm and confident as I answered her.

"There are several ways out. Let me check the plans on my lookup to work out which is closest."

I tapped my lookup, and stared at the maze of corridors. We'd taken a right turn, run past two more turnings, taken a left, and then... No, according to the plan, the left turn we'd taken didn't exist. Either I'd forgotten something, or I'd missed seeing some side turnings in the darkness. I couldn't work out where we were, or even which direction we should be going. There was a numbered door nearby, but that didn't help because there were no numbers on my plan.

I daren't tell Issette that we were lost. If we kept going straight on, then we must get somewhere eventually. If we didn't... Well, we could use our lookups to call for help, but we'd be in an awful lot of trouble.

"We go this way," I said.

I led the way down the corridor to the next junction and went straight on. At the next two junctions, we went straight on again, but at the third we had to turn left or right. I'd just decided to go right, when there was a cry of delight from Issette. I turned to look at her, and saw she was pointing to a faded sign on the wall. A fire exit sign!

We followed the sign down the corridor to the left, found another sign pointing to the right, and a corridor that ended in a red door. I waved my hand at the door release, the door opened, and a combination of heat and bright sunlight hit us as we went through it. We'd escaped!

I stopped and shielded my eyes with one hand as I looked around. We were standing outside a massive building, its grey flexiplas wall dotted with small doorways and windows. At the far end of it, I could see some much larger doors, and a huge sign saying "Earth Europe Off-world". If we wanted to, Issette and I could come back when we were 18, go in through those doors and see those ten chunky portals again. What we couldn't do, what we could never do however old we were, was walk through one of the portals.

I knew exactly what would happen if we did, because Hospital Earth allowed its wards one attempt at portalling off world when they were 14, to prove there hadn't been a mistake in diagnosing them as Handicapped. I'd been one of the very few fool enough to try it. I'd portalled from a hospital rather than an Off-world, arrived on an Alpha sector world, collapsed into the arms of the waiting medical team, and been thrown back through the portal. Things were a bit hazy for a while after that, but I remembered enough pain to make me absolutely certain I never wanted to try it again.

Interstellar portals were for the norms, not for me and my friends. Whether you called us the officially polite but sneering word, Handicapped, or the open insults like throwback and ape, didn't change anything. Every other handicap could be screened out or fixed before birth, but the doctors couldn't do anything about this one. There were over eleven hundred inhabited planets spread across six different sectors of space, but we were imprisoned on Earth. Any other world would kill us within minutes.

ALPHA SECTOR 2788 - DALMORA

Danae, Alpha sector, June 2788.

I'd had a new sari for every birthday, and they'd all been beautiful, but the one for my eighteenth birthday was truly breathtaking. It was floor length, in my favourite white and burgundy, and covered in intricate, shimmering, embroidered patterns. I twirled round, my waist-long black hair flying around me, admiring myself in the twin full-length mirrors in the corner of my bedroom, while my three younger sisters sat on my bed watching me with awe.

"You look dazzling, Dalmora," said Asha.

"Absolutely lovely," said Sitara.

"Totally zan!" cried Diya, far too loudly.

She instantly slapped her hand over her mouth, and we all turned to look at the door, holding our breath in case Mother had been close enough to hear that. After a couple of minutes, the bedroom door still hadn't opened, so we all relaxed and collapsed on the bed in a fit of giggles.

I finally calmed down, and guiltily remembered I was about to become an 18-year-old. Here on Danae, no one was considered fully adult until 25, but 18 was an important first step in growing up. The sari I was wearing, that of an adult woman rather than a girl, symbolized that. I'd be able to stand at my mother's side at her formal parties, welcoming the guests. I'd be able to apply for courses at University Danae. I'd even be able to vote, though naturally my vote would only count for half as much as a full adult.

It was totally wrong of me to encourage Diya by giggling with the others. I should be setting her a good example and helping my mother teach her the correct standards of behaviour. "You really must stop using slang, Diya," I said. "You know how much Mother hates it."

She pulled a sulky face. "It's not fair. The children in the vids I watch all use slang, and nobody nags at them."

I frowned, wondering if I should ask exactly what vids Diya had been watching, but decided it was better if I didn't know. "I expect those children live on very different worlds to ours. You mustn't get into the habit of using slang, Diya. It's not just that Mother doesn't like it; you know you'll get into trouble at school as well. The Academy is very strict about not allowing its pupils to use slang."

Diya pulled a face. "The Academy rules don't even make sense. The teachers scold us for saying amaz instead of amazing, but then they complain if we say something is interesting instead of saying interest. Why do they do that? If we're supposed to speak formal Language at all times, then saying interest or fascinate should be as wrong as any other slang."

My youngest sister had a habit of asking awkward questions. Father said it was because Diya was highly intelligent, with an analytical, enquiring mind. Mother said it was because Diya liked being difficult. Right now, my sympathies were with Mother. I hesitated, trying to think of a good answer.

"Saying fascinate is an accepted modification of formal Language used in the highest social circles in Alpha sector," I said at last.

"So Mother wants to stop us using slang that's in common usage on all eleven or twelve hundred worlds of humanity, and encourage us to use slang that's only used by aristocrats on the capital planet of Alpha sector." Diya sighed. "What's the point in that? Even if we visit Adonis, we're hardly likely to meet any Adonis Knights."

"It's not just used on Adonis," said Asha. "It's used in the first social circles here on Danae. That's why the Academy insists on us using it."

"I hate going to the Academy," said Diya.

Nobody bothered to answer that. The Academy was the finest, most expensive, and most exclusive school for girls on Danae. Mother had attended the Academy. Both our grand-mothers had attended the Academy. That meant we all had to attend the Academy as well.

Diya wrinkled her nose. "You all hate going to the Academy too, don't you?"

"It has impressive gardens," said Asha.

"But you hate going there," said Diya.

"It has fine architecture," said Sitara.

"But you hate going there," repeated Diya.

Asha and Sitara both looked at me. What could I say? The Academy was famous for its glorious flowerbeds and genuine marble pillars, but it was a miserably strict place, with people constantly watching you and criticizing your behaviour, your stance, your accent, even how you were breathing.

I did the cowardly thing, and evaded the question entirely. "I've taken my final examinations, so I'm not attending the Academy any longer."

Diya made an inelegant snorting noise that would have earned her a week's detention if any of the Academy's teachers had heard her. "But..."

She was interrupted by the sound of the clock in the hall chiming half past one. It was a totally accurate reproduction of an ancient nineteenth century clock, apart from the adjustment to allow for the length of a day on Danae being slightly different to the length of a day on Earth.

All four of us stood up, checked our appearance in the mirror, and filed out of the room. Mother was already waiting for us in the hall, so the four of us lined up facing the house portal. Mother adjusted the folds of our saris, and tidied Diya's hair, before taking her place next to us. We all looked expectantly at the portal for the next thirty seconds, then there was a series of musical notes. It was a moment before we realized they weren't actually coming from the portal, but the front door instead.

We all hastily swung round to face the door, and Mother gave the faintest of groans before speaking. "Front door command open."

The door swung open, my grandmother entered, and Mother stepped forward to greet her. "Welcome, Mother Rostha."

She paused before continuing in a pointed voice. "There's no need to arrive using the public portal outside, Mother Rostha. The house portal is set to accept your genetic code, so you can portal straight into the house."

Grandmother frowned at Mother's sari, and adjusted its folds before answering. "I keep forgetting you have a private portal. So few people find it necessary to have such a luxury."

Grandmother had said variations of this on every single one of her last ten visits. I had to admire the way Mother kept her face and voice perfectly calm as she gave her usual reply. "House portals are becoming far more common these days. Ventrak has to do a huge amount of travelling to create his history vid series, and it makes his life a little easier if he can portal straight into the house."

"My poor son works so hard to pay for your extravagances." Grandmother moved towards me and nodded her approval. "Dharma is always flawlessly dressed."

"My eldest daughter's name is Dalmora, Mother Rostha." There was the faintest edge of acidity in Mother's voice.

"Well, it shouldn't be," said Grandmother. "Dalmora is not a traditional name. I named all three of my sons after the first colonists on Danae."

The acid note in Mother's voice grew stronger. "It was Ventrak who suggested Dalmora should be named after my mother."

"My poor son has always been such an indulgent husband," said Grandmother.

Mother closed her eyes for a second, a sure sign she was losing patience. Sitara, Diya and I couldn't say a word, or we'd get a lecture from our grandmother for speaking before we were spoken to. I glanced at Asha.

"Forgive me for interrupting, Grandmother," said Asha, "but the embroidery on your sari is stunning. Can I ask if the fabric is one of your own designs?"

Grandmother turned towards her, and her forbidding expression abruptly melted into a smile. Asha was her favourite granddaughter, named after her, and always treated with special leniency. "Yes, this is my latest design. You have excellent taste, Asha. I look forward to the day you will come to me to be trained as a fabric designer yourself."

"Thank you, Grandmother." Asha gave a dutifully grateful smile, though I knew she had absolutely no interest in becoming a fabric designer. Father's history vid series, *History of Humanity*, was famous on worlds in every sector of humanity's space. Asha, Sitara, and I all wanted to make info vids ourselves one day. Diya talked about becoming a scientist, but it was impossible to tell if she was serious about that, or just saying it to be awkward.

There was another series of musical notes, this time from the portal. We all hurried to line up facing it, my mother on one end of the line and my grandmother on the other. The portal established, and my father stepped through. He looked tired, but he smiled at us, and greeted each of us in turn, before taking out his lookup to check the time. On Danae, birthdays were celebrated on the anniversary of the person's birth, using the interstellar standard Green Time of Earth Europe. Here on Danae it was early afternoon, but it was almost midnight by Green Time.

Father watched his lookup for a moment, then nodded and turned to me. "Happy birthday, Dalmora." He held out a small box. "For you to wear at your birthday party this evening."

I took the box, found it held a set of tiny rainbow lights for wearing in my hair, and gasped in pleasure. Rainbow lights were the height of fashion on Adonis, and girls were starting to wear them on Danae too, but I knew my grandmother strongly disapproved of them as being far too theatrical. I gave her a wary look, but found my father was already offering her an identical package.

"I couldn't resist getting a set for you too, Mother. Your hair has always been so beautiful, it deserves no less."

Grandmother graciously accepted her package of rainbow lights. "You are always so thoughtful, Ventrak. I look forward to wearing these at the party."

Grandmother would naturally approve of any gift from her adored eldest son. It seemed rainbow lights had suddenly become perfectly respectable.

Mother stepped towards me now, lifting her hands to undo the golden necklace she was wearing. She studied it for a moment with a reminiscent smile, then looked at me and spoke in a measured, formal voice. "One of my ancestors brought this necklace with her when she left Earth during Exodus century. It has always been handed down to the eldest daughter in the family on her eighteenth birthday. My mother gave it to me on my birthday. Now it is time for me to give it to you, Dalmora."

I felt guilty taking the heirloom from my mother, but this had been a family tradition for over five centuries now. The necklace had been made by a far distant jeweller ancestor in the city of Jaipur on Earth, to be a birthday gift for her eldest daughter. The necklace, and its story, had been passed on from daughter to daughter ever since. I had a duty to accept it now, just as I had a duty to pass it on to my own daughter when she was 18.

The necklace felt surprisingly cool and heavy as I put it round my neck. Mother helped me fasten it and then smoothed my hair back into place. This necklace was a true piece of history. Wearing it now, I knew I was just one link in a chain of owners that stretched back half a millennium into the past, and could continue as far, or even further, into the future.

Mother stepped back to admire me, and this time I wasn't surprised when Father produced a third package of rainbow lights and handed it to her. She gave him a quick smile of thanks before speaking.

"We must eat now, because Ventrak will need to rest before the formal party begins." She turned and led the way into the small reception room we used for private meals.

We all followed her and sat down around the table. Grandmother looked at the array of dishes set out, and frowned. "I'd expected Ventrak would be welcomed home with a proper hot meal."

Father shook his head. "The informal eating arrangements are entirely for my convenience, Mother. I've spent a week on Asgard in Gamma sector, consulting some of my old teachers at University Asgard about my plans for future vids, and now I have to make a seven hour time zone adjustment. I find that biorhythm adjustment meds solve the sleep problems, but sudden changes in meal patterns are still difficult."

Mother stood up. "I'd be happy to get you a hot meal, Mother Rostha, if you prefer that."

Grandmother waved a hand in dismissal. "I couldn't possibly cause you so much trouble."

Mother sat down again. Grandmother eyed the bowls of food, gave a martyred sigh, and we all started eating.

"It's so unfortunate that you studied at University Asgard rather than University Danae, Ventrak," said Grandmother. "Collaborating with history experts at University Danae would be far more convenient."

Father's smile flickered for a second. "It would be more convenient, Mother, however I've explained to you many times that I chose to study at University Asgard because its history department was more highly regarded than the history department at University Danae. I remain convinced that my contacts at University Asgard can give me far more useful assistance than anyone at University Danae."

He paused. "Since you've raised the subject of University Danae, Mother, I think now is a good time to have a discussion about Dalmora's future."

I looked at him, startled and anxious. What did he mean? My future had been decided years ago. I would continue to live at home while I studied at University Danae. Father had studied modern history, the period from Exodus century to the present day. His *History of Humanity* vid series covered key events in modern history. I was to study pre-history, the days when humanity only lived on Earth, so I could help him to make a new vid series featuring events from far in the past.

There was the question of my future husband, of course, but Danae tradition was that the subject shouldn't be discussed with me until I'd completed my degree course. I was aware my father was already bearing in mind the fact he had four daughters, and quietly choosing suitable young men of good family to assist him in his work, but...

"During my visit to University Asgard, I mentioned the fact Dalmora would be starting her history studies at University Danae after Year Day 2789, and my contacts gave me some important information." Father's voice developed an unusual edge of annoyance. "I should add that I was both surprised and disappointed that we had not been told this information when Dalmora made her application to University Danae."

He paused. "It appears that University Danae no longer runs a history degree course."

"What?" The word slipped out before I could stop it. "I'm sorry, Father. I shouldn't have interrupted you."

He shook his head. "You are understandably shocked, Dalmora. As I said, I was disappointed that University Danae chose to mislead us. Apparently the rules for history degrees have changed since I was a student. All the Foundation courses must now concentrate on pre-history and be held on Earth."

"Earth!" Grandmother frowned. "It's out of the question for Dalmora to go to Earth. It would be criminally negligent for University Danae to send their students to a world where they'd be in contact with the Handicapped."

Father sighed. "Apparently that's exactly how University Danae felt about it, Mother. They weren't allowed to accept students onto a full history degree course unless they'd completed the new Pre-history Foundation course, so they chose to replace their history degree with a degree in historical studies."

"That seems a sensible solution," said Grandmother.

"Apart from the minor detail that their historical studies syllabus includes a lot of literary and philosophical content, and virtually no pre-history," said Father. "Given Dalmora wished to specialize in pre-history..."

He sighed again. "We appear to be faced with a situation where Dalmora either has to study a largely irrelevant degree at University Danae, or apply to an entirely different university."

"Out of the question," repeated Grandmother. "Almost all universities on other worlds have mixed classes!"

"I don't consider that segregating male and female students is necessarily desirable," said Father. "I requested information on history courses at University Asgard, and they've been extremely helpful."

University Asgard! I wasn't just stunned now. I was, as Diya would say, totally grazzed. If I studied at University

Asgard, I wouldn't be living at home, or even on a different world in Alpha sector, but on the capital planet of Gamma sector. No, if University Asgard was following the new rules...

"Would that mean I'd spend my degree course Foundation year studying pre-history on Earth, Father?" I asked.

"Yes," he said. "I do have some strong reservations about that. Not because of the Handicapped issue. Medical experts advise there is absolutely no risk in spending time on Earth; all the studies prove that it doesn't increase the chance of having a child with immune system problems. My concern is that the new Pre-history Foundation course apparently includes physically demanding work, excavating the ruins of Earth's ancient cities."

"Yet again, that's out of the question," said Grandmother. "A delicately built girl like Dalmora can't be expected to perform manual labour like... like some muscular farmer's daughter on a primitive frontier world!"

Father turned to look at Mother. "I feel that this decision has to be made by Dalmora herself. My associates at University Asgard suggested I could take Dalmora to Earth and meet a lecturer who runs one of their Pre-history Foundation classes. We would then be able to discuss all our concerns with him. I think we should accept their very gracious offer."

Mother frowned, clearly worried.

"I have a history degree," added Father. "I make history vids. Now I stop to think about it, it does seem faintly ridiculous that I've never even set foot on the planet where most of human history happened."

"It's all totally impossible," said Grandmother. "If only you had a son then..."

Mother threw a single furious glance in her direction, before turning back to my father. "If you feel that's the wisest course of action, Ventrak, then naturally I agree."

Father turned to me. "Are you happy with this, Dalmora?"

"Yes, Father." I was going to visit Earth! I reached up to touch the necklace I was wearing. Long ago in Exodus century, this necklace had been around the neck of my ancestor when she left Earth. For the first time in four hundred and fifty years, it would return to the world where it was made.

Two days later, my father and I stepped out of a portal at Danae Off-world. Everyone immediately turned to look at us, or rather look at him. Ventrak Rostha, Danae's most famous son, wearing the same traditionally styled, pure white clothing that he wore in every one of his celebrated history vids. I was an insignificant figure at his side, wearing a discreetly simple sari, appropriate for travelling to other worlds.

Danae Off-world was crowded, but a clear path opened ahead of us as people moved aside to let us through. Father smiled and nodded his thanks to them all, as he walked on towards the off-world portals.

"I can never get used to this, Father," I murmured. "The way everyone stands aside for you, as if you were an ancient king walking through an admiring crowd."

"You must never get used to it, Dalmora," he said. "I must never get used to it either. Every time it happens, I have to remember that being treated like this is an honour, but also a huge responsibility. When people on any world of humanity hear the name Danae, they think of two things. The beauty of our firefly clouds, and my history vids. Wherever I go, whatever world I visit, I have a duty to always treat people with courtesy, showing respect for their feelings and customs, because my behaviour must never bring discredit on the name of Danae."

I nodded, understanding that it was a duty that didn't just apply to my father, but also to me as his daughter.

"It's not always easy, Dalmora," he added. "There are so many worlds with different attitudes and customs. I'm

fortunate that the traditional male dress of Danae is conservative enough to be acceptable on any world, but I've still
managed to make mistakes. Fortunately, people have always
been gracious enough to accept my apologies."

He glanced upwards at a sign. "There's a block portal to
Earth Europe soon, but if we wait for it there's a danger we
would be late for our meeting."

The lecturer from University Asgard was disrupting his
schedule to assist us. It would be deeply discourteous for us to
be late for the meeting, and Father was wealthy enough that
the cost of dialling a special interstellar portal link wasn't an
issue. We walked on past the queues to an off-world portal
that was deserted except for a uniformed attendant.

"Earth Europe please," said my father.

A moment later, the portal established and we stepped
through. I looked round, tense with excitement. I was on
Earth, the home world of humanity, the place where people
had lived and loved and fought their wars for millions of years
before the invention of interstellar portals and the exodus to
other worlds.

It was disappointing to see that Earth Europe Off-world
looked almost identical to Danae Off-world. The crowds of
people looked very ordinary too. I saw there were some, like
my father and I, wearing clothes in the widely varying styles of
different Alphan worlds, and a group of two women and one
man in Betan togas, possibly the members of a triad marriage.
Mostly though, people were wearing clothes that were more
like those of Gamma sector than anything else.

I realized I'd been foolish. Earth Europe Off-world was
hardly likely to look like a history vid. Father was already
following the signs to the local portals, and I hurried after
him. Not more than ten minutes after stepping through the
portal in the hall of our house on Danae, Father was dialling
the portal code given him by the lecturer from University
Asgard.

When I went through the portal after my father, I was expecting to arrive in another sadly generic public building, but instead I found we were outdoors. Twin portals stood in the middle of an area of rough grassland, surrounded by slightly higher ground. A man was sitting on a lump of weathered rock, staring at the ground with a thoughtful expression. When he saw us arrive, he stood up, turned to face us, and smiled.

"I'm Lecturer Playdon of University Asgard."

I'd expected to see someone at least as old as my father, but this man didn't look more than 30 at most, and he had a serious air about him that was oddly attractive.

"I very much appreciate you taking the time to meet us," said Father.

"That's not a problem," said Lecturer Playdon. "I'm a great admirer of your *History of Humanity* vid series, and the way it has given so many people an appreciation of the importance of modern history."

I felt he genuinely meant the words, but there was something strangely reserved about his manner when he said them. I'd watched a lot of people meet my father for the first time, and it was usually obvious that they were struggling to control their excitement, but this man seemed as disappointed by us as I'd been by Earth Europe Off-world.

"Thank you." Father gestured at me. "This is my daughter, Dalmora."

I fought the urge to press my hands together in the traditional greeting gesture of Danae. I was on Earth, which predominantly followed Gamma sector customs, and this man was from a Gamma sector university. That meant I should either smile or shake hands in greeting. I'd been taught at the Academy that shaking hands showed more respect, but Father said it was always best to follow the lead of the person on their home ground. Lecturer Playdon had just smiled rather than holding out a hand, so I did the same.

"Welcome to Earth, Dalmora," said Lecturer Playdon. "My superiors at University Asgard tell me you're considering applying to one of our Pre-history Foundation courses, but you're worried about the conditions students face. Since I teach a Foundation class myself, I'm to answer your questions and reassure you about any concerns."

The way he was studying me seemed almost disapproving. Did that mean I should have shaken hands after all, or did he suspect I'd demand special treatment on a Foundation course because my father was famous? Of course I wouldn't do that. It would be completely unfair to other students.

Then his words sank in properly, and I realized I was already getting special treatment. Lecturer Playdon had obviously been ordered to drop everything to meet us and answer our questions. That explained his lack of pleasure in meeting my father, and his manner when he looked at me. He admired my father's vids, but he was disappointed by our behaviour.

I felt both embarrassed and deeply ashamed, but I remembered my Academy training, and the stern lecture our deportment teacher had given me last year. "Feeling embarrass- ed is acceptable, Dalmora. Allowing other people to see you are embarrassed is not. Showing your embarrassment is pure self- indulgence, because it makes other people feel uncomfortable."

I fought to get myself under control. Luckily, Lecturer Playdon was talking again rather than waiting for an answer from me. "It's perfectly sensible to want more information about the conditions on our Pre-history Foundation course. Most of our students don't give it a moment's thought."

I had half a second to hope that meant he wasn't thinking too badly of me after all, before he continued. "They don't even bother to read all the detailed course information. They assume Earth is like any other world, and they'll be living in standard student accommodation. They get quite a shock when they see the truth."

Now I wished I could sink into the grass-covered ground and vanish forever. I'd known I'd had a privileged lifestyle, attending a fine school, living in a luxurious home and wearing expensive clothes. I hadn't thought it had affected me as a person, but I was wrong. Father said we should always treat others with courtesy and respect, but I was taking up a lecturer's time to get information when I hadn't even spent five minutes looking up the course details.

It wasn't that I'd been too lazy to do it, I'd just never thought about it, but that seemed even worse. Had I grown so accustomed to having everything handed to me that I couldn't even think for myself any longer?

"The course information says that a class is allocated accommodation in a dome near the ancient city they are studying," said Father. "What is that accommodation like?"

"I'm afraid the accommodation is very basic," said Lecturer Playdon, "with a class of thirty students and their lecturer packed into a single dome. Given those students come from widely differing planets and cultures, sharing the dome can be a learning experience in itself. The actual work is hard too. Hours of gruelling excavation work each day, more hours of lectures, and even more time working on assignments."

Father was frowning now. "I'm not sure that would be suitable."

Lecturer Playdon sighed. "However, I've been told that, given your long and mutually beneficial relationship with University Asgard, there could be certain exceptions to the rules in Dalmora's case. The residency requirement could be waived to allow her to arrange her own accommodation and portal to the dome each day. She could also be excused all but minimal excavation work."

I could tell by his expression that Lecturer Playdon had been ordered to say that. His superiors at University Asgard were prepared to make concessions to get the daughter of

Ventrak Rostha to join one of their courses. Lecturer Playdon hated offering those concessions, and my father...

I glanced at my father and saw he was hesitating. I knew he'd have strong moral objections to such an offer. He'd certainly never accept anything like it for himself, but for one of his daughters...

He started speaking. "I admit that would ease the..."

Interrupting my father in mid-sentence was shockingly bad behaviour. I did it anyway, because I mustn't let him compromise decades of perfect integrity to save me a little discomfort.

"Lecturer Playdon, if I join a course it has to be on exactly the same terms as everyone else. Living with students from other sectors would be a great opportunity for me to learn more about their cultures, and the excavation work is surely an integral part of the course. One day, I hope to help my father make a new vid series, covering events from back in the days of pre-history, so it's essential I learn as much as possible about Earth and its ancient cities."

Lecturer Playdon stared at me for a moment, then something almost imperceptible about his body language changed. I felt as if I'd passed a test and been approved.

"That's an admirable ambition, Dalmora," he said. "I'd very much like to see a *Pre-history of Humanity* vid series."

He paused. "You've probably been wondering why I asked you both to meet me here. My class is currently working on London Main Dig Site, but you can't go near the ruins without special protective clothing. Please follow me."

He turned and led the way up a rise in the ground. We followed him and I found myself on a hilltop looking out across...

"All those ruins are London?" I asked in awe. "Stretching as far as I can see?"

He nodded. "We're on top of Parliament Hill, the highest point in London. They deliberately left this area free from buildings, and there's no especially hazardous wildlife round here, so we're safe enough in ordinary clothes."

I was still staring into the distance, totally amazed. "So big. So impossibly big."

"Humanity may never build such cities again," said Lecturer Playdon. "Once you have portal technology, and can travel instantaneously around a planet, you don't need cities any longer, but London dates from thousands of years before the invention of portals."

"Thousands of years." I repeated the words. "The first settlement on Danae was built four hundred and fifty years ago in 2338."

Lecturer Playdon laughed. "We think there were scattered settlements in this area even before the days of written records. The city itself was founded 2,800 years ago by the Romans. I'm sure they came to stand on this hill and look at the view, just the way we're doing now."

I looked down at the ground in wonderment. "This was part of the original Roman Empire? Interest!"

"Yes," said Lecturer Playdon. "During the second century, 60,000 people lived in this city."

I shook my head. "So London was a bigger city then, than any settlement we have on Danae today!"

"Yes, but then the Roman Empire declined, and the city was almost abandoned at the end of the fifth century. By the sixteenth century, it had grown again to about 50,000 people, and then..." Lecturer Playdon shrugged. "The cities every-where grew bigger and bigger after that. We think London housed about ten million people at its peak. The invention of portals halved the population of all the cities, and then came interstellar portals and people headed for the stars."

He pointed. "You see that huge, ruined, dome-shaped building?"

I nodded.

"This morning, my class were excavating near there," he

said. "We found several items. I'd been told your family had an heirloom necklace, and I see you're wearing it now."

"Yes," I smiled. "It was made over five centuries ago in Jaipur."

"This is several centuries older than that." He handed a gold ring to me. "A wedding ring. The engravings show it was made in London in 1941."

I studied the circle of gold, and wondered about the human story behind it. How many people had worn this ring, and why was it left behind when London was abandoned? Surely someone leaving Earth could have taken something so small with them. Perhaps it had belonged to a dead relative, and they felt it was more appropriate for it to stay on this world.

"Your students found this ring?" I asked. "Could I help find something like this myself one day?"

Lecturer Playdon nodded. "You could."

I handed the ring back to him. "That would be an amazing experience. I realize we're interrupting your work, and we shouldn't keep you from your class any longer, but I'm very grateful to you for meeting us. It's been truly fascinate!"

"I'm always happy to assist a student with a genuine interest in history." Lecturer Playdon gestured back towards the portal. "I'm afraid I can't leave visitors here alone. This spot is safe enough, but it's still technically part of London Main Dig Site, so…"

I took one last look out across London, wondering if Jaipur was anything like this, and then Father and I turned to walk back to the portal. When we reached it, Father thanked Lecturer Playdon again, and then we portalled back to Earth Europe Off-world. We started walking back towards the interstellar portals.

"I can't believe I've never spared a few hours to visit Earth before," said Father. "I wish we could stay for a day or two, but I have a series of meetings arranged in Beta sector.

Fortunately, I have the impression you've already seen enough to make your decision, Dalmora."

"Yes, Father," I said. "I wish to apply to University Asgard and study pre-history here on Earth."

"What you said about University Asgard's offer... I'm proud of you, Dalmora. You showed true integrity."

I felt myself blush. "Thank you, Father, but I would like you to make one special request to University Asgard on my behalf."

"Yes?"

"University Asgard runs several Pre-history Foundation course classes," I said. "If possible, I would like to join one run by Lecturer Playdon."

BETA SECTOR 2788 - LOLIA

Artemis, Beta sector, October 2788. Since I'm trying to avoid any spoilers for Earth Girl, there are only vague hints about one important detail in this story. People who've already read Earth Girl should know exactly what that detail is.

Part I

Last month, I'd celebrated my twenty-fourth birthday surrounded by smiling family and friends. Last week, I'd been happily dreaming of the future. Yesterday, I'd been part of a loving triad marriage.

Today, my dreams and my marriage had been shattered, and I was sitting alone in a room. Ten minutes ago, the older of my two husbands, Ardreath, had left, slamming the door behind him. My mind was still reeling, not so much from the way he'd slapped my face, but from his final, brutal words.

My great-uncle, Lolek, had often told me I was too emotional, and maybe he was right. My pain was as bad as if Ardreath had carved those words into my skin with a knife.

I couldn't believe this was really happening. Ardreath couldn't have said those things. Ardreath couldn't have hit me. The only possible explanation was that I was having a horrible nightmare.

So I sat there, numbly staring at the closed door, willing

my nightmare to end. When it did, when I woke up, I'd tell Ardreath and Lolmack about the ghastly dream I'd had. They'd hug me, and laugh at me for being so silly, and life would go back to normal.

A chiming sound made me jump. I turned to frown at the lookup I'd left lying on the table. It chimed again, and then a third time. I stood up, went over to pick it up, and saw Ardreath's image flashing on the screen.

I had a sinking feeling in my stomach even before I answered the call. Getting a call on my lookup was entirely too realistic for a dream.

Ardreath's face appeared on the lookup screen, and he started talking in an icy voice. "Lolia, I've formally registered my divorce from our triad marriage. You should receive the official confirmation notice within the next day."

"What?" I urgently shook my head. "You can't do that, Ardreath. You can't!"

His eyes weren't looking at me, and he kept talking as if I hadn't said a word. "I've withdrawn exactly one third of the funds from our joint credit account, and removed my name from the apartment tenancy agreement. Any future communications to me should be sent via my clan's legal representatives."

The call abruptly ended. I finally understood that it hadn't been a proper call at all, but a recorded message. Ardreath hadn't had the guts to look me in the eyes and say he'd divorced me.

"Nuke you!" I screamed at the blank screen of my lookup. "Nuke you!"

I stood there, shaking with anger for a moment, and then slumped back down in my chair. I couldn't pretend this was just a bad dream any longer. Ardreath had divorced me, and Lolmack... Where the chaos was my other husband, Lolmack? He seemed to have vanished.

I tapped at my lookup to call Lolmack, then hesitated at

the last moment. Our triad marriage was broken, so Lolmack would have to choose between me and Ardreath. If Lolmack blamed me for what had happened, took Ardreath's side over this and divorced me too...

I was in no state to cope with yet another devastating blow, but I couldn't bear sitting and waiting in uncertainty either. I gnawed my lower lip in indecision for a moment, before grimly going ahead and making the call. If Lolmack was dumping me too, then it was better to know it right away. Clinging to false hope would only make things harder in the end.

But Lolmack didn't answer my call. I waited a minute, two minutes, then stabbed my lookup with my forefinger to cancel the call. There was no point in trying to force Lolmack to talk to me. The fact he wouldn't even answer my call told me everything I needed to know.

I stared down at my clenched fists. I had to face up to what was happening. Ardreath had divorced me. Lolmack had disappeared and wouldn't answer my calls, which meant he'd chosen Ardreath rather than me. I should have known he would. Ardreath and Lolmack had been lovers before I even met them. They were going to stay together now. They were going to blame everything on me, blank me out of their lives, and carry on together as if I'd never existed.

Painful memories of our wedding day came into my mind. The sound of our voices exchanging our vows. I'd been so quiet that I'd had to repeat some of the words because people couldn't hear me the first time, and Ardreath had seemed surprisingly nervous too, while Lolmack was totally calm. Anyone would have thought that Lolmack was the one who was three years older than the other two of us, not Ardreath.

When Ardreath and Lolmack's divorces were finalized, and both of them were legally free of me, there'd be another wedding, but this time it would be a duo marriage not a triad. I pictured them with their arms round each other, laughing happily, while I stood watching them, alone and bereft.

I winced at that image, and then a host of trivial secondary worries came flooding in. What about our furniture? What about the vid script Lolmack and I were in the middle of writing? What about...?

I felt sick thinking of the dozens of mundane things that would have to be done to disentangle my life from the lives of Ardreath and Lolmack, but at least I didn't have to cope with them alone. There would be plenty of people to help me, because I was part of the sprawling extended family of a Betan clan.

It was true that my clan wasn't important or historic. We were just a small clan cluster of the lowest social rank, which had been formed less than forty years ago by a group of clanless families. We didn't live on one of the powerful Betan worlds like Zeus or Romulus either. Artemis had been great once, but had been hit by disaster over a century ago.

None of those things mattered. The key benefit of the clan culture of Betan worlds was that your clan would always be there to support you through any crisis. I only needed to call for help, and my clan would come to care for me.

I reached for my lookup. It was patterned with images of flowers, an incongruously frivolous thing to use to tell people dreadful news. I frowned at it, wondering who to call first, then realized the stupidity of making individual calls. Saying this once was going to be painful enough. I couldn't force myself to repeat it over and over again.

I set my lookup to record a message. "Hello, everyone. I'm afraid I have b-b-b-bad news to..."

I broke off and bit my lip. I thought I'd broken myself of my stammer when I was a teenager, but it was back. I couldn't deal with that on top of everything else, so I took the easy way out, summed up the nightmare of the last twenty-four hours in a text-only message of three brief sentences, and sent it to my whole clan.

An incoming call came barely three minutes later. I didn't even look to see who was calling, just answered it, and was startled to see the rigidly autocratic face on my lookup. My great-uncle, Lolek, our head of clan!

"Great-uncle!" I said. "It's very kind of you to call me yourself, but it really wasn't necessary. I…"

He ignored that. "You have blood on your face, Lolia. What happened?"

I'd known my cheeks felt wet, but I'd assumed that was from my tears. I instinctively touched my left cheek with my hand, and then studied my fingers. Yes, there was some blood among the tears.

"Ardreath slapped me," I said. "He wears the latest fashion in chunky jewelled rings, and one of them must have scratched me. I didn't notice or I'd have washed it off and…"

"No!" Lolek interrupted me. "Don't touch your face. Don't move. Don't talk to anyone. We'll be with you in a few minutes."

He abruptly ended the call. I stared at my lookup in bewilderment. I hadn't expected my great-uncle to call me himself, or to care about a simple scratch on my cheek. He'd said the words "we'll be with you," so he must mean he was coming to visit me himself. I hoped he'd only stay for a moment, and then leave my parents and friends to help me.

It shouldn't take Lolek more than five minutes to go to our clan hall portal, dial the right code, step through, and walk the remaining short distance to my door. I tensely watched the time on my lookup, aware that I must look an awful mess after the way I'd been crying. I desperately wanted to wash my face, redo my makeup, and brush my hair, but Lolek had told me not to touch my face. Lolek could get very angry if his orders weren't strictly obeyed.

It was much longer than I'd expected, nearly twenty minutes, before there was a soft chiming sound from the door. I stood up, and took a deep breath to try and calm my nerves. "Door command open."

The door opened and I stared in confusion as people flooded into the room. Lolek was in the lead, but behind him weren't my parents or the friends I'd expected. Instead, there were a couple of my older cousins carrying cases of vid equipment, and several strangers.

No, at second glance I saw these weren't actual strangers. The two men and one woman might not be clan members, but I had seen them before. The woman was our clan doctor, one of the men belonged to the law firm we used, and the other was our clan image consultant.

The doctor hurried up to me. "Please sit down, Lolia," she said.

I sat back down in my chair. The doctor waved a scanner at me, concentrating on my face, before turning to Lolek.

"Only very minor bruising and a superficial scratch."

"But it's still legally second level assault," said the lawyer. "Under Betan law, any drawing of blood automatically escalates an assault from first to second level. Use of a weapon would escalate it even further to third level, but it would be extremely hard to argue a fashionable ring counted as a weapon."

The image consultant was studying my face now. "We could use more blood for the vid."

My two cousins had finished unpacking vid bees from their carrying cases. Lolena picked up a makeup bag, and came over to me. I felt her dabbing some liquid on my face, while my other cousin watched critically.

"I wouldn't overdo it," he said. "I know face wounds bleed a lot but..."

"I'm not overdoing it," said Lolena. She stepped back and studied me for a second. "Perfect."

"We'll need Lolia crying in the vid," said the image consultant.

Three small, spherical vid bees floated up into the air, and hovered across to me. I saw their lights flash as they focused on me and started recording. What the chaos was going on here? Our clan business was making vids, but why were they making a vid of me?

I finally got over my shock enough to speak. "What's happening?"

Lolek turned to glare at me. "What's happening?" He repeated my words in a mocking voice. "What's happening is we're trying to limit the damage you've done to the clan, Lolia."

I shrank back into my chair. "Damage? Me?"

"Are you completely brainless or merely totally self-centred?" Lolek gave an impatient sigh. "Ever since I formed this clan, I've been working towards getting us official recognition and a true clan name. Surely even you must understand that an important step on that path is to be in an alliance with clans who already have official status."

He didn't wait for me to reply, just swept on. "I spent years trying to negotiate our way into an alliance without success. We're wealthy, so an alliance might have accepted us despite the fact we're a mere clan cluster, but given our wealth comes from making what most of Beta sector regard as vulgar vids for export to other sectors..."

He shrugged. "When you got involved with Ardreath and Lolmack two years ago, I knew we had a golden opportunity. Ardreath belonged to the Eastreth clan, which was in an alliance of nearly thirty respectable clans, headed by the Breck clan of the middle rank. More than that, Ardreath was the adored son of the Eastreth clan leader, who indulged the boy's every whim."

Yes, Ardreath had always been handed everything he wanted. Lolmack and I had often joked about it, but the jokes didn't seem funny any longer. If Ardreath hadn't had such an easy life, he might have reacted differently to the current crisis.

"The Eastreth clan leader wanted to indulge his son this time too," said Lolek, "but he was faced with a big problem when Ardreath started talking about marriage to you and Lolmack. You belonged to a disreputable clan cluster. Lolmack, Mack as he was called back then, was even worse. A totally clanless nobody with a criminal record. The Eastreth clan council were prepared to consider solving the problem by adopting you, but they turned up their noses at the thought of adopting Mack as well."

I remembered the arguments between Ardreath and his father back then. His father had suggested Ardreath should just marry me and forget Mack entirely. Ardreath had snapped back that Mack was the centre of our triad relationship. I'd been hurt by Ardreath's words at the time. Something about the way he said them sounded as if he only wanted Mack, and I'd been forced on him as an unwelcome third.

Ardreath had laughed when I said that, told me I was being silly and of course he loved me as much as Mack. I'd believed him then, but now I wondered if he'd been lying. Perhaps our triad marriage had been flawed right from the start, doomed to break apart as soon as we hit a problem.

Lolek was still talking, indulging himself with a smug smile of reminiscence. "So I negotiated a solution. The Eastreth clan would get us into the Breck alliance, increasing our clan's status. We'd adopt Mack into our clan as Lolmack during the marriage ceremony. It was perfect for all of us."

His smile abruptly vanished. "It *was* perfect, Lolia, but you've messed everything up now. Our clan was admitted into the Breck alliance because of your marriage to Ardreath. Now that marriage has broken down, there's every chance the Eastreth clan will demand we leave. They've been members of the alliance since it was first formed sixty years ago. Our clan has only been in the alliance for two years. Who do you think will win that battle, Lolia?"

I stared at him. "B-b-but I haven't done anything wrong. Ardreath is only b-b-blaming me b-b-because..."

"And stop that childish stammering!" shouted Lolek. "Didn't those expensive hours of speech therapy achieve anything at all?"

I took a deep breath, and used the tactics my therapist

had taught me. Speak with deliberate slowness, avoid contractions, and imagine you're reciting a poem. "I am very sorry this has happened, Great-uncle, but I did not do anything wrong."

"It's your fault, Lolia. We'll lose our place in the alliance. We'll lose our chance at being recognized as a true clan." Lolek's words hammered relentlessly at me. "We'll lose everything, and it's *all your fault!*"

"But I did not do anything wrong!" I wailed the words yet again, and there was a moment of silence. I felt tears streaming down my face, and gulped for breath between sobs.

"That's it!" said the image consultant. "Play me a clip of her face just then."

A holo image of my head and shoulders appeared in midair. I was cowering in my chair, literally shaking in distress, with mingled blood and tears streaking my cheeks.

"That's perfect!" said the image consultant.

Lolek nodded at the vid team. "Exactly what we needed. Send the vid clip to my lookup and pack up your equipment. We're done here. I..."

He was interrupted by a bleeping sound. Lolek reached for his lookup, glanced at it, and pulled a face. "As I feared, the Eastreth clan have called an emergency meeting of the alliance council. They'll have told them about the marriage breakdown, but they won't have mentioned Ardreath hitting Lolia. They probably don't even know about it. Ardreath must realize his clan would strongly disapprove of such behaviour, as both dishonourable and illegal, so it's quite possible he hasn't admitted it to them. If he hasn't..."

Lolek put his lookup away and gave a cold smile. "If he hasn't told them, then we still have one chance."

He turned to me. "Give me your lookup, Lolia!"

"What? Why?"

"Your lookup, Lolia," he repeated impatiently.

I handed it over.

"The doctor will care for you now. She'll take you to a secret location where Ardreath's clan can't find you, and she'll check all your incoming calls for you. That way you won't be distressed by anyone, or tricked into saying something that you shouldn't." He passed my lookup to the doctor.

I shook my head. "A secret location? Where? Why can't I go to our clan hall?"

He ignored my questions. "Remember, you're to do exactly what the doctor tells you, Lolia."

"I want to talk to my parents," I said.

He ignored that too, turned, and went out through the door. The image consultant and lawyer hurried after him, followed by the vid team. I was alone with the doctor.

Part II

I sat there for a moment, silently absorbing what had just happened. All of my life, I'd been terrified of my great-uncle. When I met Ardreath and Mack, I'd been stunned by the way Lolek suddenly abandoned his usual stern, disapproving manner and started smiling at me. For a while, I'd even thought he genuinely cared for me.

Now I knew I'd been right to start with. Great-uncle Lolek had started smiling at me back then, because he could use me to help his inter-clan political manoeuvring. Now I'd turned into a hindrance instead of a help, there were no more smiles. He hadn't even...

I felt something cold against my face and instinctively recoiled.

The doctor sighed. "Please hold still, Lolia. I have to clean your cheek, and put a fluid patch on it."

"But I don't need a fluid patch for a simple scratch."

She sighed again, finished cleaning up my face, then produced a fluid patch from her medical bag. She held it to my cheek and activated it. The ridiculously over-sized patch clung to my skin, and the newly released regen fluid made my whole face feel icy cold. This must be like the extra blood for the vids, intended to make it look as if Ardreath had seriously injured me.

I was tempted to rip the patch off, but then I remembered the things Ardreath had said to me, and the recorded message he'd sent. Let Lolek cause Ardreath all the trouble and embarrassment he could. He deserved it!

The doctor closed her bag and picked it up. "We have to go now, Lolia."

I shook my head. "I can't go outside looking like this. I need to fix my makeup, my hair, pack my things, and..."

"We have to go right now," repeated the doctor. "There's no need to worry about your things. Someone will pack all your belongings and bring them to us."

"But..."

"Now, Lolia!" ordered the doctor. "Representatives of the Eastreth clan may arrive at any moment. Your head of clan will be very angry if they manage to talk to you."

I reluctantly stood up and followed her to the door. I realized I didn't even know this woman's name, but I didn't bother to ask it. I resented Lolek putting her in charge of me, giving an outsider, a member of a different clan, the right to order me around.

"Where are we going?" I asked as we went outside.

"A very comfortable hotel."

"I'd rather go to my clan hall."

"I'm just following the instructions of your head of clan, Lolia." The doctor marched on at a rapid pace. "He said it would be easier to control the situation this way."

We only passed two people on the way to the nearest portal. One was standing still, studying his lookup, so totally absorbed in the shimmer vision holo display floating above it that he didn't even notice us walk by. The other gave the fluid patch on my face a single startled look before hurrying on.

The doctor dialled the portal code, blocking my view of it with her body. I wasn't sure if that had been deliberate or accidental. Either way, once the portal established and we stepped through it into a hotel foyer, I had no idea where I was. The inhabited continent of Artemis was very long and thin. I could be in a hotel in the western highlands, the eastern marshes, or near the great rift itself. I automatically reached for my lookup to check my location, before I remembered the doctor had it. It felt oddly frightening to be somewhere unknown, cut off from the universe without my lookup.

The doctor led the way down a corridor to a door labelled 36, pressed her hand on the door plate, and it opened. "Room command lights," she said.

Concealed glows came on, filling the room with a medley of coloured lights. The doctor led the way inside, giving an approving nod at the furnishings. "Very nice."

I was less impressed. The room was comfortable enough, but the glittering wall decorations were a type that had gone out of fashion before I was born. I wouldn't have been happy with any hotel room though, however modern and luxurious. I didn't want to be in a hotel. I wanted to be in my clan hall with my parents and friends.

The doctor opened doors to reveal two bedrooms, and a food dispenser. "Would you like something to eat, Lolia?"

I gave her a disbelieving look. "You expect me to eat reconstituted food from a food dispenser?"

"I know your clan is extremely wealthy, but you must surely have eaten food from a food dispenser when you were a student."

I'd eaten plenty of meals from food dispensers when I'd been studying at University Artemis, and most of them hadn't been that bad, but I looked the doctor in the eyes and lied. "Of course I didn't. Give me my lookup, so I can order some cartons of real food."

She shook her head. "I can order them. What would you like?"

I listed a few random dishes, and watched sourly as she used her own lookup to order them. By now I was positive she'd deliberately blocked me from seeing our portal destination, and that whatever excuse I invented she wouldn't let me touch my lookup. I didn't like what was happening here. I didn't like it at all. I wasn't just being hidden from Ardreath's clan; I was being cut off from my own.

Lolek had told the doctor that it would be easier to control the situation like this. I had a feeling he really meant it would be easier to control me.

The food cartons were delivered to our door, and I made an attempt at eating, then two people arrived, the same two cousins who'd made the vid of me earlier. They had a whole set of hover bags floating behind them.

"We've brought all your things, Lolia," said Lolena. "I'll help you with your hair and makeup."

She opened one of the bags, and got out my makeup case and my best formal toga.

"I'm supposed to look respectable now instead of a terrified victim?" I asked. "What's going on? Why do I need a toga? Are we going to a formal clan meeting?"

Lolena ushered me to a chair. "The alliance council meeting is currently in session, and Lolek is showing them the vid we made of you after Ardreath's attack. They may summon you to appear next. If they do, we want you to appear calm and immaculately presented, except for the fluid patch on your cheek. The alliance council members will compare your current appearance with your devastated state in the vid. The contrast should convince them of the brutality of Ardreath's attack."

I frowned at my reflection in the mirror. Despite all the other emotions already churning around inside me, I managed to feel panic at the idea of appearing before an alliance council meeting.

"Don't wrinkle your forehead like that!" Lolena scolded me. "You'll ruin your makeup."

She worked on my hair and makeup with professional speed and skill, and was just helping me into my toga when her lookup chimed. She glanced at it and nodded. "You're wanted now, Lolia. Follow me quickly, because alliance council won't like being kept waiting."

She hurried out into the corridor, and headed for the portal. I chased after her in a panic. "What do I have to say?"

"As little as possible," she said. "Lolek will give you your cues."

My cues? Everyone kept acting as if we were making a vid, and I should obediently follow the script I was given, but this was real life, this was *my* life!

When we reached the portal, Lolena dialled our destination. She didn't bother to hide it from me, there was no point because I knew exactly where we'd be going. The Breck clan headed the alliance, so alliance council would be meeting in the Breck clan hall.

When we stepped through the portal into a corridor, I saw Lolek standing there waiting for us, wearing the white toga with thick gold edging that proclaimed his status as a head of clan.

"Lolia, listen carefully," he said. "I was right about Ardreath. He hadn't told his clan about hitting you. When I made the accusation, Ardreath's father, Arden, denied it. I then showed alliance council the vid of you. Arden accused me of faking it. I challenged him, demanding both you and Ardreath should face a truth test, and he had no choice but to agree."

A truth test? But what if I was asked about the fluid patch, or...?

"During the test, you must only answer my questions," continued Lolek. "Don't be drawn into responding to anything Ardreath or Arden says to you. Our clan's position in the alliance depends on you following my instructions exactly. Do you understand?"

I gulped and nodded.

"And don't shame our clan by stammering!" said Lolek.

He turned and swept off down the corridor. I followed him, glancing over my shoulder for Lolena, and saw her vanish off through the portal.

When I faced forward again, I discovered Lolek had stopped by some ornate double doors. I barely managed to avoid bumping into him, and he gave me a scathing look before lifting his right hand into the air.

The double doors opened in response to his gesture, and we went through them into a huge room. I saw a circle of gilt chairs, holding about thirty men and women in formal togas. Three chairs were bulkier and more imposing than the rest. The two women and one man in those chairs would be from the Breck clan. The other people must be the leaders of the other clans in the alliance.

Lolek sat down in the single empty chair, and I saw him look across the circle at where Arden Eastreth Calvart, the head of the Eastreth clan, was sitting. I felt a stab of pain when I saw Ardreath standing behind his father's chair, looking classically handsome in an elegantly draped toga.

"The girl has no right to wear a toga," said Arden. "Togas may only be worn by members of officially recognized clans. Now my son has registered his divorce, the girl has returned to her original status as a gutter clan brat."

He paused. "In fairness though, she is merely following Lolek's example. He has no right to wear his toga either."

Gutter clan brat! I lifted my head and glared at Ardreath. Yesterday, I'd been his wife, and now he was standing there, calmly listening while his father insulted me! I knew I mustn't say anything, but...

"Both Lolia and I wear togas to show proper respect for the alliance council," said Lolek calmly. "If alliance council prefers, then we will happily remove them."

"Unnecessary," said the woman seated in the centre of the three Breck clan chairs. I'd seen enough images of her, to instantly recognize the formidable Marissa Breck Thane. Despite rejuvenation treatments, her skin was delicately lined with age, and her black hair had threads of silver in it. That meant she was over 80, automatically entitled to respect in age conscious Beta sector, but Marissa Breck Thane would be treated with respect anyway. She'd been the Breck clan leader, presiding over meetings like this, since before I was born.

She turned to look at Arden. "An alliance council meeting

should be a dignified affair. You will refrain from petty insults and deliberate provocation."

"I apologize," said Arden, "but you must surely understand my anger at this situation. Lolek has made false accusations in front of the entire alliance council, accusing my own son of second level assault on a woman, and producing a fake vid as evidence. Such behaviour cannot be tolerated in this alliance. The gutter clan must go!"

Marissa Breck Thane lifted her hand to stop him. "For the second time, and for the formal record, I warn you to refrain from further use of insults, particularly the word 'gutter.' You will follow the convention agreed by alliance council to deal with the issue of having a clan in the alliance that has no true clan name, and use the phrase 'Lolek's clan.'"

Arden reluctantly bowed his head in acceptance.

"Two years ago, you argued the case for admitting Lolek's clan to this alliance," continued Marissa Breck Thane. "They made vids, so their business interests were in line with those of the alliance, but given those vids were of a low class nature designed solely for the export market..."

There was a meaningful pause before she continued. "Alliance council had reservations but finally agreed to your request. The admission of Lolek's clan has, on the whole, been advantageous to the alliance, opening up new export opportunities, but now you demand we expel them."

She pulled a face. "You have said we must understand your anger at this situation. Equally, you must understand our displeasure. Marriages between members of alliance clans have broken down before, and the resulting issues have been resolved amicably even when complex business mergers and property transfers had been linked with the marriage contract. It has never been necessary to remove a clan from the alliance."

"This case is very different," said Arden. "Lolek's accusations have pushed things beyond the point where an amicable resolution is possible. Clan Eastreth isn't formally allied with the reactionary faction, but we agree with their protective attitudes to women. My son would not do something as dishonourable as assaulting any woman, let alone one who was, at that time, his own wife!"

"This alliance is formed around common business interests," said Marissa Breck Thane in an icy voice. "Alliance council's position on politics is strictly neutral. Your reference to reactionary attitudes to women is, at a minimum, inappropriate. Given reactionary views on women holding positions of authority in clans, it could even be regarded as insulting to the female members of alliance council."

Her right forefinger twirled in the circular gesture that meant the same thing on every Betan world. The discussion was over. Arden's expression was that of a man who knew he'd just made a big mistake.

"Let it be formally recorded that the Eastreth clan refuse to withdraw their demand for the expulsion of Lolek's clan," said Marissa Breck Thane. "Both clans have agreed to submit this entire issue to the judgement of alliance council rather than involve outside officials."

That didn't surprise me. The Eastreth clan would find a police investigation embarrassing, because they were highly respectable. My clan would find a police investigation embarrassing, because we weren't respectable at all, and couldn't afford to have officials nosing around some of our more questionable business affairs.

"We've heard more than enough accusations and denials," continued Marissa Breck Thane, "so the witnesses will now take the stand and we will establish the true facts."

Lolek caught my eye, and gestured at one of several large metal discs in the centre of the room. I walked between the chairs and went to stand on the disc, and was taken by surprise when a second, much smaller, metal disc hovered up to float in front of me.

"Put your right hand on the disc, Lolia," said Lolek.

I put my hand on the disc, and the pulsing blue light of a scanner appeared. When I looked up again, I saw Ardreath was standing on a matching disc, facing me. I fought the urge to turn away, staring straight into his eyes instead. I'd done nothing wrong. He was the one who'd broken our marriage, not me.

Marissa Breck Thane took a moment to study both of us. "Alliance council will be basing its judgement on the Betan laws regarding assault. Given the relative sizes of the two participants, I think we can ignore the legal exemptions for brawls involving equally matched and willing parties."

There was a ripple of laughter from the clan leaders.

Marissa Breck Thane nodded at Lolek. "You may establish the truth of your accusation."

"Lolia, did Ardreath hit you?" asked Lolek.

I smiled coldly at Ardreath, and was pleased to see the panic in his eyes. I carefully chose my words to avoid the letter "b," because that was always the most likely to trigger my stammer. "Yes, he hit me."

"Scans show that Lolia is almost certainly telling the truth." Marissa Breck Thane turned to Arden. "You may counter the accusation."

Arden frowned. "Ardreath, did you hit the girl?"

Ardreath looked down at the blue light scanning his right hand. "I may have accidentally touched her."

"And Ardreath's statement is definitely not true," said Marissa Breck Thane. "I would advise him to stop wasting alliance council's time with lies, because such behaviour will count against both him and his clan."

Ardreath took a deep breath. "Yes, all right, I lost my temper and hit Lolia, but Lolek's accusation of second level assault was a lie. I didn't do anything that would draw blood. That vid Lolek showed you, with Lolia's face covered in blood, was a fake."

"Now Ardreath is speaking the truth," said Marissa Breck Thane. "Lolek, please respond to his point about the blood."

"Of course," said Lolek. "Lolia, did Ardreath's jewel-encrusted ring cut your face and make it bleed?"

"Yes, it did," I said.

Ardreath gave me a startled look, which changed to one of pure apology. He'd been my husband for two years. Despite Lolek's orders, I couldn't stop myself from responding to his contrite expression.

"I'm sure Ardreath didn't intend that to happen," I added. "He turned round and left immediately afterwards, so he probably never saw the blood."

"And that statement is also true," said Marissa Breck Thane. "I believe we have now established the real facts. Does anyone have any additional questions for the witnesses?"

She waited a moment, glanced round the circle of clan leaders, and nodded. "The witnesses may stand down."

I went back to stand behind Lolek's chair. As I walked by him, he gave me a single harsh glare, before returning his attention to Marissa Breck Thane. She was on her feet now, looking solemnly around the circle of clan leaders.

"Lolek's clan made an accusation of second level assault against a member of clan Eastreth. Clan Eastreth claimed the accusation was false and countered it with a demand for the expulsion of Lolek's clan. The accusation has now been proved to be true, but it appears clan Eastreth had had genuine reason to believe it false."

She paused. "In any other case involving such a misunderstanding, I would ask both clans to reconsider their positions at this point. In this case though, given the scale of ill feeling demonstrated, I feel alliance council has no choice but to debate whether the continued presence of both clan Eastreth and Lolek's clan in our alliance is either desirable or possible."

Marissa Breck Thane sighed. "Expelling either or both of

these clans would be a serious matter, with significant business consequences for many alliance clans, so clan leaders will wish to consult with their clan councils before voting. Alliance council will therefore continue with the debate this evening, but votes will not be cast until tomorrow morning. It is obviously inappropriate for the leaders of the two clans concerned to be present during either the debate or the vote. They will be summoned in the morning to hear alliance council's decision."

Lolek and Arden both stood up, bowed to the Breck clan leader, and then turned to leave. Lolek was closest to the door, so he went through it first, with Arden behind him. I followed after them, and found myself walking down the corridor next to Ardreath. I was startled to hear him whisper to me.

"I apologize for hitting you. I was under extreme stress, but it was still an indefensible action."

I hesitated, and glanced at Lolek and Arden. They were deep in conversation with each other, speaking in low pitched angry voices, so I whispered back to Ardreath. "Our marriage doesn't have to end like this. Perhaps it doesn't have to end at all. A couple of days ago, the three of us were so happy. We could be like that again."

Ardreath gave me a fleeting, sad smile, before his expression hardened into something cold and calculating. "You've always been such an endearingly naive child, Lolia. Many marriages are just about people and emotions, but some are heavily involved with finances and politics as well. Two years ago, my clan had badly underestimated the cost of a business expansion. Your clan was extremely wealthy and could give us the bridging loan we desperately needed. In return, we could negotiate your entry into our alliance."

I stared at him. "You're saying you only married me to get a loan for your clan?"

"Hush." Ardreath pointed a warning finger at Arden and Lolek. "Our marriage benefited both our clans, and it was an attractive prospect personally as well. You're an eye-catching girl, and Mack… He and I had already been together for a year at that point, but my father was totally opposed to our relationship. Understandably so. Mack wasn't just clanless, but a convicted thief."

Somehow those words angered me even more than the comment about marrying me to get a loan for his clan. "You know the truth about that theft conviction as well as I do. Mack was barely 15 years old back then, and trying to find a way to escape that ghastly orphanage on Janus."

"Yes," said Ardreath, "but my father and my clan council were naturally unhappy about Mack having a criminal record. I told them that you wouldn't marry me unless you could marry Mack as well, and that no marriage would mean no bridging loan."

He shrugged. "They gave in after that, and the arrangement worked very well for everyone concerned. My marriage to you and Mack was a slight social embarrassment for my clan, but the money compensated nicely for that until one of my clan's vid series became a runaway success and solved our financial problems."

He paused. "Then, yesterday's… unfortunate event occurred. My clan council lost patience, and threatened me with being made clanless unless I divorced the pair of you. In those circumstances, I really had no choice but to end our marriage and distance myself from you both."

I glared at Ardreath. I thought I'd been a fool not to work out that Lolek was using me as a pawn in his political games, but I'd been even more stupid than that. Ardreath's clan had been using me to get a bridging loan, while Ardreath had been using me to get his clan to consent to him marrying Lolmack.

I opened my mouth to tell Ardreath to nuke off, then realized the implications of his last sentence. "You're not planning to start a new marriage with Lolmack then?"

"That would be impossible in the circumstances. I'm deeply unhappy about that, but…"

Ardreath broke off. Arden had glanced over his shoulder, and made an impatient beckoning gesture. Ardreath hurried to join him, and Arden turned back to face Lolek.

"The loan will be repaid in full by tomorrow."

"With interest, I hope," said Lolek.

Arden nodded. "With interest."

He and Ardreath hurried on to the portal, dialled it, and vanished. I wondered what Arden would be saying to Ardreath now they were alone. Arden had trusted his son to tell him the whole truth, and now his clan leader position might be in jeopardy. The Eastreth clan council would be furious when they heard Ardreath had misled them.

Whether Arden hung on to power or not, Ardreath would be in a lot of trouble, but I didn't care what happened to him any longer. My mind was totally focused on one thing. Lolmack wasn't with me, and he wasn't with Ardreath either, so where the hell was he?

"Idiot girl!" snapped Lolek.

I turned to face him, but I was still thinking about Lolmack.

Lolek gave me a withering look of contempt. "Aren't you capable of following the simplest instructions? We had the Eastreth clan totally defeated, we could have driven them out of the alliance, but you had to open your stupid mouth and say Ardreath probably didn't see the blood. Now alliance council will use the excuse that the Eastreth clan honestly misunderstood events to keep them in the alliance and discard us instead."

He paused for a second. "If there's any way at all of staying in the alliance, our clan must take it. If there are demands that we remove potential sources of future conflict between us and clan Eastreth, we must agree to them. You understand what that means, Lolia?"

I nodded. Oh yes, I understood exactly what he meant. This whole argument was centred on my failed marriage.

Removing a potential source of future conflict, meant removing me. Lolek was saying he'd happily sacrifice me to safeguard the clan's position in the alliance.

"You will return to the doctor, and remain with her until we hear alliance council's decision." Lolek dialled the portal and waved at me to go through.

I stepped through into the hotel foyer and found Lolena waiting for me. She didn't say a single word, and seemed to be trying not to look at me as she led me down the corridor. Had Lolek warned her about the situation? Was she already making the mental shift from thinking of me as family to thinking of me as a clanless outsider? Would the rest of my family and friends discard me as lightly?

Now I knew exactly why I'd been isolated in a hotel suite rather than allowed to return to the clan hall. The second Lolek heard about my marriage breakdown, he'd considered the option of removing me from the clan. He knew it would be hard to do that if I was staying at the clan hall with my friends and family around me, but no one could contact me here. No one knew what had happened or where I was. Lolek could make up any story he wanted to get people to accept his decision.

Lolena dutifully delivered me to the hotel suite and then left. I was alone with the nameless doctor again.

Part III

The doctor gave me a look of professional concern. "You've had a very stressful day, Lolia. You should try to get some sleep."

Sleep? How could I sleep at a moment like this? At a word from the alliance, my clan would discard me. I'd lose my family. I'd lose my friends. I'd lose my job too, because I worked for the clan business.

How the chaos could I survive alone, clanless, and with no income? I had a degree in Art of Language from University Artemis, and I was a good vid script writer, but most of the Artemis clans who made vids were members of the Breck alliance. Their clan leaders had been in the alliance council meeting, where I was the centre of a storm that threatened the unity of the alliance. They'd never give me a job after that.

In fact, getting any sort of job would be desperately hard. In Beta sector almost every business was owned by a clan. They all employed their own clan members in preference to anyone else, second choice was members of clans in their alliance, and then members of other respectable clans. The clanless were only employed as a last resort, because everyone assumed they must have done something dreadful to be disowned by their clan.

I'd never had to worry about money before. I wasn't just paid a generous amount as a script writer; I could ask for help from the clan funds as well if there was any unexpected emergency. Now though...

All I had was my share of the money that Ardreath, Lolmack, and I had in our joint credit account. That might last for two or three months if I was very careful, but what would I do after that? I was vaguely aware that it was possible to get a subsistence grant if you had no other income, but I didn't know how much it was or how you claimed it.

I remembered Lolmack's stories of the orphanage on Janus. My guess was that subsistence grants would be exactly like that orphanage, the absolute grudging minimum provision given with as much humiliation and bullying as possible, because things like subsistence grants and orphanages were only for the clanless. Any clan with a shred of pride cared for its own members rather than let them ask for help elsewhere.

"Take this." The doctor held out a glass of water and a tablet. "It will help you sleep."

I didn't need to sleep. What I needed was my lookup, and there was an obvious way to get it. "I'd rather have some juice. I think there was a carton left earlier. I'll get it."

I found the carton, collected two glasses from the food dispenser, and filled them both with juice. I carefully put my tablet in my mouth between my teeth and my cheek, drank from one of the glasses, and swallowed the juice but not the tablet.

The doctor smiled, apparently totally satisfied. "You'd better go and lie down now. Which bedroom would you like?"

I yawned, covering my mouth with my hand for a moment. "Do they both have this dreadfully old-fashioned glittery decor?"

The doctor went over to open a bedroom door and look inside. "This one has, but it's a very nice shade of delicate pink."

The tablet was in the palm of my hand now. "I hate pink. What's the other one like?"

The doctor went to check the second room. I dunked the tablet into the untouched glass of juice, and rubbed it between my fingers. I felt it soften, but it stubbornly refused to dissolve.

"Blue," the doctor reported.

"I prefer blue." I yawned again. "Can you put my bags in that one please?"

The doctor collected the key fob that controlled the set of

hover luggage, clicked it, and the bags floated into the air and followed her into the bedroom. I had another desperate attempt to make the tablet dissolve in the juice, and this time I succeeded. I peered into the depths of the juice. Fortunately it was bright red, so any remaining fragments of tablet were invisible.

I left the full glass of juice on the table, and carried my own half-empty one into the bedroom, moving slowly as if I was already half asleep. The doctor met me, and hastily took the glass from my hand, putting it on the table next to the bed.

"Shall I find you a sleep suit?" she asked, gesturing at the hover luggage.

"No, I... I'll lie down now, and change later."

I stretched out on the bed, and closed my eyes. There were a couple of minutes of total silence, followed by what I thought was the sound of the doctor leaving the room.

I opened my eyes cautiously and looked around. Yes, the doctor had gone. Silly woman, letting me fool her like that. Had she forgotten that my clan made vid programmes? Given the type of vids they were, I didn't act in them myself of course – my clan hired the clanless or outlanders from other sectors as actors – but I'd still learned a lot about acting over the years.

The question now was if the doctor would drink the juice and be drugged by her own tablet. I hoped she would. If necessary I was prepared to hit her over the head with her own medical bag, but it would be a lot easier for both of us if she just drank the juice.

I made myself wait what seemed like an endless time, but was probably only half an hour, then crept across to the door and opened it a crack. The doctor was sitting in a chair, slumped to one side, apparently deeply asleep. On the floor beside her was the empty juice glass.

My theory was that the doctor would have given me a very strong sedative to make sure I didn't cause trouble, but I was still careful not to make a sound as I entered the room. I remembered seeing the doctor put my lookup in her medical bag, so... Yes, it was there!

I grabbed it, retreated back into the bedroom and closed the door, then eagerly checked for messages. There were some from my parents and friends, all saying roughly the same thing. Lolek had told them I wanted to be left alone to recover, but I should let them know if I needed anything. I got the impression everyone was worried about the situation, but too scared of Lolek to argue with him.

I got to the end of the messages and bit my lip. The message I wanted most was missing. There was nothing at all from Lolmack. I frowned. My parents and friends had tried to call me, and left messages when they didn't get an answer. It was possible Lolmack had called me too, but not felt able to leave a message. If he was as uncertain about my feelings as I was about his...

I remembered my lookup kept a log of calls, and hurriedly checked it. There was a whole list of entries with Lolmack's name! The first call must have arrived only minutes after the doctor took charge of my lookup. There were a dozen more after that, and several attempts to send recorded messages as well. Everything was flagged as automatically rejected. The doctor must have set my lookup to reject any contact from Lolmack.

I cancelled the reject order, and tapped the lookup to call Lolmack myself. There was a long delay, and I started panicking, thinking that after making so many rejected calls he'd decided to reject mine, then he finally answered.

I felt a sudden surge of emotion at the sight of his face. Lolmack wasn't nearly as handsome as Ardreath, but I'd always felt so safe with him to protect me. Even talking to Lolek hadn't been as frightening when Lolmack stood next to me. Just looking at him now made me feel reassured and...

But I mustn't let myself feel like that. I mustn't start counting on Lolmack, not until I knew...

"Lolia!" Lolmack had obviously been lying down when he answered the call. His image juddered for a moment as he sat up, and brushed his hair out of his eyes with his left hand. "Sorry to be so slow answering. I was fast asleep."

Fast asleep? I was surprised because it was still early evening.

"I missed your last call because it came when I was portalling," he continued. "You know how going through a portal completely confuses the call system. I've been trying to call you back ever since, but the calls kept being rejected."

I pulled a face. "That's because Lolek took my lookup."

Lolmack seemed to hesitate for a moment, then nodded. "I guessed it was something like that. Lolek sent me a message telling me I was banned from the clan hall, and would be removed from the clan as soon as clan council had time to meet, so I knew he wouldn't want you contacting me. Where are you now?"

"Lolek left me at a hotel with a doctor guarding me. I've drugged her, and got back my lookup, but I don't know how long the drugs will last."

Lolmack looked at me blankly for a couple of seconds, before his expression changed to a mixture of surprise and amusement. "You drugged someone?"

"Yes. A lot has been happening here. I'll explain it all later, but..."

"What happened to your face?" he interrupted me. "Did Lolek hit you?"

I'd forgotten about the fluid patch on my cheek. "No, it wasn't Lolek. Ardreath slapped me, and caught me with one of those fancy rings he wears. It was only a slight scratch, but Lolek insisted on me wearing a fluid patch to make it look bad in front of the alliance council."

I pulled off the fluid patch. "See, my face is already healed. Forget about that. The important thing now is..." I desperately needed to know if Lolmack still wanted me, still cared about me, but I was scared to ask in case I got the wrong answer. "Ardreath said he'd divorced both of us."

Lolmack paused before replying. "Yes, I got a cowardly recorded message from him." He laughed. "Isn't it absolutely typical of Ardreath's credit counting soul that, even in the midst of disaster, he remembered to take a third of the funds from our joint account before he divorced us?"

I would have laughed too, but I was too nervous. "So... Where does that leave us?"

Lolmack kept me in suspense while he thought about that, then he raised an eyebrow. "Where does that leave us? Ardreath may have dishonourably broken his vows and left our marriage, but I have not. Unless you choose to end our marriage, Lolia, you remain my wife. Always."

I felt a weird floating sensation as relief hit me. I forced it away. If Lolmack and I were going to be together, I had no time to waste. "Then I'll come and join you right away. What's the code for your nearest portal?"

"Joining me could be a little difficult," said Lolmack.

"What? Why?" For a moment I'd thought everything was all right, Lolmack still wanted me, but maybe he didn't after all. The way he kept hesitating, thinking things over very carefully before he said a word...

"I'm not on Artemis any longer," he said.

Lolmack wasn't on Artemis! Now I understood the delays before he responded to the things I said. He hadn't been hesitating or thinking things over. He was on another world in a different star system, so my call was being relayed through a series of comms portals to reach him and there'd be a short delay before he heard what I said. That explained why he'd been asleep too. He must be on a world where it was night time.

"Did Lolek force you to leave Artemis?" I asked.

Lolmack laughed. "Both Ardreath and Lolek made it clear in their messages that I wasn't welcome on Artemis any longer, but that's not why I left. Ardreath's threats don't scare me. He likes to think he's tough, but he's been raised as a member of a highly respectable clan. He'd have no idea where to hire thugs to beat me up, and he wouldn't last five seconds in a fight with me himself."

I shook my head anxiously. "I know Ardreath isn't a real danger, but Lolek…"

Lolmack had a habit of using a negligent, relaxed manner as camouflage, but now he let the mask slip to look blatantly lethal. "It's amusing that Lolek thinks he could just order the clan enforcement group to attack the man who's been their leader for the last year, and they'd instantly obey. The truth is that they wouldn't openly defy Lolek, but they'd make very sure they kept looking for me in the wrong places."

Lolmack shrugged and adopted his usual lazy posture again. "But it's irrelevant anyway. Lolek's power is strictly limited to Artemis, so I'm safely out of his reach now."

I was less sure about that. Lolek had agents on some of the nearer Betan worlds, who helped with some of our clan's more dubious business activities. "Where exactly are you?"

"I'm on Earth, of course." Lolmack smiled. "I have family here."

He was on Earth! Even when I was picturing what life would be like alone and clanless, it had never occurred to me that I could leave Artemis, let alone leave Beta sector. It wasn't something a Betan would ever consider doing, but Lolmack hadn't been born in Beta sector. He'd lived on a dozen different worlds before he came to Artemis as a 16-year-old orphan.

"How do I get to Earth?" I asked.

"You're seriously considering joining me on Earth?"

I nodded. It hadn't occurred to me before, and even if it had I'd have been too scared to do it alone, but with Lolmack…

"Do you realize how your clan would react to you coming here?" asked Lolmack.

I pulled a face. "My clan may be discarding me anyway.

There's a battle going on over whether we stay in the alliance, and Lolek is willing to do anything to win it."

Lolmack made a sound of disgust. "The clan discarding me is understandable. I'm just a stray they adopted, but you're their own blood raised in their own clan hall. Have they completely forgotten their oaths as Betans? Loyalty to family comes first and foremost in that oath."

"It's Lolek deciding this, not the clan."

"No, it isn't," said Lolmack. "Under Betan clan law, a clan leader can't expel a clan member by himself, he needs clan council's agreement as well."

"Betan clan law only applies to officially recognized clans. Lolek follows the rules when it suits him, but when it doesn't..."

"It's more than time the clan stood up to Lolek, told him that they won't accept his dictatorship any longer. If they won't defy him over expelling you, then when will they do it?"

I couldn't say anything. I didn't trust myself not to break down.

Lolmack made a horizontal, air-slicing movement with his left hand, the classic Betan gesture of rejection. "Nuke the clan. Lolia, it would be wonderful if you joined me here, but think carefully before you decide. You've never left Artemis before, Earth is a dreadfully prudish world, and its people are prejudiced against Betans. Moving here would be a huge culture shock for you, and we wouldn't be able to afford the luxurious lifestyle you're used to."

I didn't need to take time to think. Yesterday, I'd been happy with Ardreath and Lolmack and my dreams for the future. This morning, I'd thought I'd lost everything, but now...

I refused to mourn over losing Ardreath, because a Cassandrian skunk would make a better husband than him. Lolmack was as solidly honourable and trustworthy as I'd always believed. I'd go to Earth and join him, and together we'd find our dreams again.

"I don't care about prejudice; I've had people sneer at me

all my life because of my low class clan. I don't care about luxuries either. I care about the people I love." I found the key fob for my hover luggage, and clicked it. The bags obediently gathered up to follow me. "How do I get off world?"

Lolmack choked back a laugh. "If you want to go off world, Lolia, the first step is to go to Artemis Off-world."

"Oh yes." I joined in his laughter. "I should have known that, but it's been a very long day. I'll call you again in a few minutes."

I ended the call, used my lookup to check the portal code for Artemis Off-world, and then opened the bedroom door. I tiptoed through the room, passing the sleeping doctor, and my luggage floated through the air after me. I'd never noticed the sound of hover bags before, but now they seemed to be humming very loudly. The doctor didn't stir though; whatever was in that tablet must have been very strong.

For a second, I was worried I'd killed her, but then commonsense prevailed. The tablet I'd given her had been intended for me. Lolek might banish me from the clan, might even murder me in the right circumstances, but he'd never involve a respectable outsider doctor in anything criminal. There'd be far too high a risk of her giving evidence against him.

I went out into the corridor, hurried to the nearest portal, and dialled. A moment later, I was in a huge hall packed with people. I suddenly thought of something very bad, gulped, and called Lolmack again.

"I'm in Artemis Off-world, but I've just realized that Lolek could find out where I was by tracking my lookup."

"He could," said Lolmack, in a reassuringly calm voice, "but he won't bother tracking your lookup when he thinks your prison warder of a doctor still has it. By the time he finds out that she doesn't, you'll be perfectly safe in a different star system. Can you see a sign for Romulus?"

I looked up at glowing overhead signs. "Yes."

"Beta Sector Interchange 3 is on Romulus. Most of the Artemis Off-world traffic goes via there, so there's usually an interstellar portal locked open for Romulus. Join the queue and go through. Call me again when you get there."

I followed the sign for Romulus and saw a group of people in Military uniforms ahead of me. The history of Artemis was literally burned into its landscape, so no one could ever forget it. Like everyone who'd been born and raised here, I had an instinctive reaction to the sight of a Military uniform. A hundred and thirty years ago, Ceron Augustus had nearly destroyed Artemis, but the Military had saved us. The presence of the Military meant security, safety, protection from any danger.

I hurried to catch up with the Military group. If Lolek had discovered I was in Artemis Off-world, and sent some of the clan to drag me back to my hotel prison by force, I could start screaming I was being kidnapped and the Military would defend me. Nothing as dramatic as that happened, of course. I just followed the Military group through an oddly bulky portal and arrived on Romulus.

I automatically moved out of the portal arrival zone, checked my hover luggage had followed me, and then looked round. I was in a building almost exactly like the one I'd left, the people hurrying by were dressed the same as people on Artemis, but the signs overhead said that this was Romulus Off-world. I'd left my home world behind me. My clan and I were in totally separate star systems now.

It took me a couple of minutes to recover from the enormity of that thought, and the exuberant rush of relief that followed. I felt horribly guilty rejoicing over being so far from my parents and friends, but it was wonderful to finally escape from under Lolek's shadow.

I called Lolmack and smiled happily at him. "I made it! I'm in Romulus Off-world!"

"Good. You should see some signs pointing the way to Beta Sector Interchange 3."

"I see them." I followed the signs down a wide corridor. "Earth is in Alpha sector, isn't it?"

Lolmack laughed. "That's right. Now I've checked the schedules, and you need to go to the waiting area for Cross-sector Gate 4. The next block portal from Beta Sector Interchange 3 to Alpha Sector Interchange 6 will be opening at Gate 4 in twelve hours' time."

"Twelve hours!" I frowned. I was impatient to reach Earth, to feel Lolmack's arms holding me close, and twelve hours seemed an eternity.

"There are often very long waits to join a cross-sector block portal, Lolia. The special portals able to handle cross-sector distances are hugely expensive, and establishing the portal connection takes a vast amount of power. Their block portal windows have to be carefully scheduled for maximum efficiency, sending through as many travellers as possible in the time."

"Oh." I thought that over. "Would taking a different route be faster?"

Lolmack shook his head. "Your only other option would be to make a whole series of short interstellar portal jumps to reach Alpha sector. That would take days, so it's much better to wait and use the cross-sector portal. Once you get to Alpha Sector Interchange 6, you shouldn't have to wait long for a block portal to Earth Europe."

"Earth Europe?" I asked, totally confused. "There's more than one world called Earth?"

Lolmack laughed again. "Other worlds have a single inhabited continent, Lolia, but Earth has five. It's simplest if you come directly to Earth Europe, so you don't have to worry about inter-continental portalling."

I sighed. "I'm incredibly clueless."

"You're incredibly brave," said Lolmack. "You've never gone anywhere alone before, you don't have the faintest idea about interstellar travel, and you know nothing about Earth, but you aren't letting any of that stop you joining me."

"You really mean that?"

He smiled. "I really mean it. Now, you look utterly exhausted. There should be a rest zone in the waiting area for Gate 4, so go there and try to get some sleep. You can dream about tomorrow when we'll be together again."

He paused. "Until tomorrow, Lolia."

"Until tomorrow, Lolmack," I said.

Part IV

When I woke up, I saw I was surrounded by sleeping strangers. I sat up in alarm, then remembered I was in the Gate 4 rest zone. I'd expected it to have private cubicles with proper beds, but it had turned out to be just a side room filled with chairs, and with big signs on the wall reminding everyone to set their lookups to silent mode.

You could adjust the chairs to a reclining position, but they still weren't very comfortable. I hadn't expected to be able to sleep at all, but I must have done. I reached for my lookup to check what time it was, and blinked in surprise. I'd been asleep for ten hours!

That meant I only had two more hours to wait for the block portal to Alpha sector. I clicked the key fob for my hover luggage, and the bags floated after me as I headed for the food dispensers in the main waiting area. They had a range of hideously overpriced breakfast cartons, and I carefully chose one of the cheapest. My journey to Earth was terrifyingly expensive, so I had to save every credit I could on other things.

The contents of the carton were very basic, but I told myself that I had to adapt to a less luxurious life now, and ate everything except an especially soggy toasted wafer. After that, I set my lookup to mirror mode, checked my appearance, and shuddered.

As a member of a clan that made vids, I'd been raised to be constantly aware of my appearance. I'd been born with a fairly average face, except for high cheek bones and an overlarge nose. My clan had had my nose corrected when I was 15, altered my hair colour from a nondescript brown to dramatic blonde, and given me training in how to use makeup to make the best of my features. Since then, people had generally thought me very attractive, but right now I resembled an Artemis ferret!

If I'd looked anywhere near this bad in my calls to Lolmack, then it was amazing he hadn't screamed and told me to stay on Artemis. I hunted through my hover bags to find my makeup case, and spent over an hour in a shower room, trying to make myself look as beautiful as possible despite the dreadfully minimal facilities available.

After that, I went back to the endless rows of chairs, and sat tensely listening to a series of announcements coming through the overhead speakers. Gate 4 must have a block portal window open to Gamma sector at the moment, because all the announcements were about Gamma sector worlds.

Finally, I heard the words I was waiting for. "Cross-sector Gate 4 is now dialling Alpha Sector Interchange 6."

I stood up.

"Travellers for Adonis should move to the departure zone now," said the announcer. "Adonis only please. Other travellers should remain in the waiting area until called."

I dutifully sat down again. The waiting area had been crowded with people, but about a third of them were heading off down the corridor labelled "Cross-sector Gate 4 Departure Zone."

After a couple of minutes, the announcer spoke again. "Travellers for destinations other than Adonis please return to the waiting area immediately or you will incur a penalty charge. Travellers to Adonis have priority because they need to reach Alpha Sector Interchange 6 within the next fifteen minutes to join their ongoing block portal to Adonis."

A trickle of people returned to the waiting area. I smothered a laugh at their embarrassed faces. It was another ten minutes before I heard the announcer's voice again. "Travellers for Earth Europe and Earth America should move to the departure zone now."

I clicked my key fob, and headed down the corridor to the departure zone. The corridor widened out and I joined a slow moving queue of people. A uniformed security guard stepped forward to speak to me.

"Have you portalled cross-sector before?"

I shook my head. "Only interstellar from Artemis to Romulus."

"Cross-sector portalling is a little different," she said, "because we have to keep the time taken per traveller to a minimum. When you're told to go through the gate, you must move immediately or you'll incur a penalty charge. Due to the sheer distance of the portal jump, you may arrive feeling dizzy, but try to keep moving clear of the portal arrival zone. If necessary, a security guard will assist you."

She glanced at my trail of hover luggage. "You've got a lot of bags there. Keep clicking your key fob to keep them grouped close to you, or some of them could be left behind. If there's free time at the end of the block portal window, we may be able to send through any lost luggage, but we can't guarantee it."

The security guard moved on to talk to another traveller. I counted my luggage, seven bags, and thought rapidly. I had plenty of dresses, so I could cope with losing a few. The vital thing was...

I opened one of the hover bags, and took out my precious makeup case. If I carried it myself, then it couldn't be left behind. The woman ahead of me in the queue was opening a hover bag as well, and taking out a fluffy toy. She smiled at me, and pointed at the little girl at her side. "It would break her heart if she lost this."

I nodded, and we all shuffled forward as the queue moved. There was a man ahead of the woman, and he turned and picked up the little girl, so I guessed they were a family.

A couple of minutes later, the three of them headed through the cross-sector gate. That was a truly strange looking portal, with peculiar extra attachments and lights, but I daren't spend time studying it. I had to keep my eyes on the security guard standing next to it, keep clicking my key fob, and be ready to...

"Now!" The security guard waved his arm.

I gave my key fob a last click as I stepped through the portal. I instantly felt sickeningly dizzy, and dropped the key fob, but someone grabbed it, took my arm, and towed me forward.

"All right?" asked a male voice with the distinctive drawling accent of Alpha sector.

The world stopped spinning. I blinked and focused on the face of a male security guard. "I think so."

"Welcome to Alpha sector." He let go of my arm, and clicked my key fob before returning it to me. "You've got seven hover bags here. Is that everything you had with you?"

I looked for my makeup bag, discovered I was still holding it in my left hand, and nodded.

"Where are you going?" asked the man.

"Earth Europe."

"You want Interstellar Portal 8 then," he said. "The next block portal to Earth Europe opens there in twenty minutes."

"Thank you."

The guard hurried off to help another arrival. I saw everyone else was moving off down a corridor, and was following them when my lookup chimed. I expected it to be a call from Lolmack, so I moved to stand by the corridor wall and answered it, but it was Lolek!

"Lolia!" He seemed startled that I was answering my lookup myself. "Why did the doctor...? Never mind, that doesn't matter any longer."

He obviously thought I was still in the hotel with the doctor. Either she was still asleep, or she'd been too scared to contact him and tell him I'd escaped. I told myself I had no need to be afraid of Lolek now I was in Alpha sector, but I still nervously checked there was only an anonymous wall behind me so Lolek couldn't tell where I really was.

"I was just summoned to hear alliance council's decision," he continued in rapid, eager tones. "My impression is that opinion was evenly divided during the debate, so the closing speech by Marissa Breck Thane decided everything. The alliance have deep respect for her opinion."

He paused with the air of someone about to give momentous news. "You read her, Lolia. I freely admit I thought you were being stupid last night, but you'd read Marissa better than I had. When she spoke this morning, giving alliance council's verdict, she said she was struck by the way you hadn't just told the truth, you'd even given details that could count in clan Eastreth's favour. She said that gave the alliance the best possible chance of finding an amicable solution, demonstrating our clan was willing to put the long-term interests of the alliance ahead of our own immediate benefit."

He gave me a smile of pure jubilation. "Our clan is to stay in the alliance, Lolia! Even better, alliance council ruled that the Eastreth clan could only remain in the alliance if Arden publicly apologized to both of us for his insulting behaviour."

He laughed. "Well, Arden couldn't stomach doing that, so he decided to withdraw the Eastreth clan from the alliance."

I blinked. How would the Eastreth clan council react to that? If Arden lost his position as clan leader, Ardreath might be made clanless. For a second, I pictured a clanless Ardreath wanting to rejoin me and Lolmack. The three of us could be together, just like before.

But no. Things could never be like that again. I'd seen the true, coldly self-centred Ardreath hidden under his charming, handsome exterior, and I didn't want him back.

Lolek laughed again. "Arden seems to have convinced his clan that Marissa and the alliance council ruled against them because they disliked their reactionary leanings. The Eastreth clan have announced they're going to join one of the reactionary faction political alliances."

I was hugely relieved that Ardreath and his father had survived the crisis. I didn't want Ardreath being made clanless and coming to ask me for help. I wanted him to remain happily with his clan, stay out of my life, and never bother me ever again.

"That means a complete victory for us, Lolia!" said Lolek. "No one will hold the Eastreth clan leaving the alliance against us, because they've done it in a way that has offended everyone. We aren't in the alliance through the charity of another clan any longer, but in our own right. That's all because of you. I'm impressed. I'm really impressed. I'd no idea you had such political acumen. You can't be a clan council member until you're 30, but I want you to attend future meetings as an observer."

I stared at him in disbelief. I wasn't going to be made clanless any longer. I could turn around, join the next cross-sector block portal back to Beta sector, and have my old, secure life back.

No, I corrected myself, it wouldn't be my old life, it would be better. I would be one of Lolek's favourites, destined to be a member of clan council one day.

I pictured that and shuddered. I'd finally escaped from Lolek, and I wasn't going back to live under his rule again.

"You are to return to the clan hall at once," said Lolek. "Marissa Breck Thane wants us to visit her tomorrow. Since Arden refused to apologize to us, she..."

"I'm afraid I can't do that," I interrupted.

Comms portal relay lag meant that Lolek kept talking for a couple more seconds before he reacted to my words. He stared at me. "What?"

"Please give my regrets to Marissa Breck Thane. Tell her that I deeply appreciate her invitation, but I can't visit her because I'm on my way to Earth."

"You're on your way to... You can't do that!"

Lolek looked as if he was about to explode. I had a very disrespectful thought about how messy it would be if he did.

"With all due respect," I said, "you forfeited your right to give me orders when you told me you would discard me from the clan. I now feel entitled to make my own decisions, and I've decided to go to Earth."

I'd never seen Lolek totally speechless before. I smiled at him. "Tell Marissa Breck Thane that I'm going to Earth because I have family there, and an honourable Betan is loyal to family above all else." I paused. "I think you'll find she understands and possibly even approves."

I ended the call, hurried on down the corridor to a huge open area, and saw a sign for Interstellar Portal 8. I followed that and joined a queue by a flashing sign that said "Earth Europe block portal opening in 9 minutes."

I reached for my lookup and called Lolmack. "I'm in Alpha Sector Interchange 6, and my block portal to Earth Europe opens in..." The time on the sign changed. "In 8 minutes."

"What are you wearing?" asked Lolmack.

"What am I wearing?" I repeated, bewildered. "The same clothes I was wearing to appear before alliance council." I held my lookup at arm's length so that Lolmack could see them.

"I warned you Earth was dreadfully prudish," he said. "They have laws about covering legally private body areas. Fortunately your toga does that, but try to remember you aren't allowed to talk about those body areas either. That means you can't say words like breast or butt in public. You can't say hell or nuke either. You have to sedately say chaos instead."

"That's ridiculous."

He shrugged. "I know, but just about everywhere outside Beta sector has the same silly rules."

"If they're so stuffy, why do they keep buying our vids?"

Lolmack grinned. "Because they're horribly hypocritical. They publicly disapprove of Beta sector because of our triad marriages and revealing clothing, but they furtively watch Betan vids in private. Are you sure you don't want to change your mind about coming to Earth?"

"I'm not changing my mind. Will you come and meet me at Earth Europe Off-world?"

He smiled. "I'm already there waiting for you."

I ended the call, looked up, and saw the person ahead of me in the queue, a boy of about 18, had turned round and was staring at me. Before I could decide how to react, the older woman with him tugged at his arm and gave him a fierce frown. The first few words she said didn't make any sense at all to me, and nor did the boy's reply, so they must have been speaking the dialect of some other sector, but then the woman swapped to Language.

"You mustn't look at that girl," she said. "She's wearing a toga, which means she's Betan!"

"I know," said the boy. "I was only..."

"Keep your eyes away from her!" said the woman. "You know what Betans are like, always trying to seduce people."

I blinked. The woman was presumably the boy's mother. Did she think I was deaf, did she think that Betans didn't understand the official common tongue of humanity, or did her home sector not believe in basic courtesy?

I opened my mouth to politely point out that the style of toga I wore was that of a married woman, which meant I had no desire to seduce anyone outside my marriage, but the woman gave a sniff of disgust that was pointedly aimed in my direction.

Now I finally realized that the woman had deliberately swapped from her home sector dialect to speaking Language because she wanted me to understand what she was saying. She wanted me to feel ashamed of being Betan. Well, I wasn't ashamed. I might have issues with Lolek's bullying rule over our clan, I might have chosen to leave Beta sector, but I was still proud of its culture and history.

The woman hadn't made me feel ashamed, but she had made me feel angry! Since this rude, narrow-minded and stupid outlander insisted on treating me like a sex-mad predator pursuing her son, I'd do exactly what she deserved and act like one!

I gave the boy a deeply suggestive smile. "Hello, gorgeous boy."

He responded with a look of temptation mixed with terror. "Hello."

His mother gave us a single horrified glance, grabbed the boy's arm again, and physically dragged him off to the back of the queue.

I laughed and faced forward again. The flashing sign changed to say the block portal to Earth Europe was now open, and the queue started moving. I saw the travellers immediately ahead of me now were a couple with a little girl, and recognized them as the same family I'd met in the queue for Cross-sector Gate 4. They all looked very happy, and I felt it was the best possible omen for the future.

I followed them through the portal to start my new life on Earth.

GAMMA SECTOR 2788 - KRATH

Asgard, Gamma Sector, June 2788.

I was humming to myself as I drove my heavy lift sled across the scrap yard, manoeuvred it into position, locked the glowing beam on to the twisted wreckage of an old digging machine, and lifted it upwards to reveal my precious hoard of...

My hum abruptly stopped. "What the chaos?"

I stared in outrage at the blank area of ground. There should have been seventy-nine crushed cubes of metal there. I'd spent over two weeks collecting them, ready to execute my grand plan this afternoon while my dad was visiting friends. The idea was to carefully position the cubes in front of our house, so when he came home he'd find them spelling out the words "Nuke off!", but the whole lot had gone.

I slapped the control to cut the lift beam. The digging machine dropped back to the ground, and I waited a moment or two for it to stop rocking from side to side, then jumped down from my sled and started roaming round the scrap yard. Perhaps my stash of cubes had been moved behind the heap of old transport sleds in the corner, or...

But no. My metal cubes weren't anywhere to be seen. I gave up, tapped at my lookup to access the yard sales system, and saw the hideous truth. My dad had sold every single one of my metal cubes this morning!

I sat down on the carcass of a dead food dispenser and sighed. This was just typical of my life. I never had any fun at all. Other 17-year-old boys went to school, made friends, met girls, while I was stuck working on my dad's scrap yard all day.

Fifteen months ago, leaving school had seemed a great idea. I'd lived on nine different planets before my dad and I moved to Asgard when I was 14. When Dad decided to settle down and start a refuse collection and recycling business, I'd thought I'd finally be at a school long enough to make proper friends, but all the other kids had known each other for years and I didn't fit in. When they found out my dad collected all the school rubbish, things got really bad. Everyone kept making fun of me, calling me scrap boy and telling me to empty the rubbish bins. I complained to a teacher about it, but the other kids all ganged up on me, denying saying anything at all, so...

Well, when Dad said that I could legally leave school at 16 to start an apprenticeship with his business, I'd grabbed at the chance. Now I was starting to think I'd made a big mistake. Nobody called me names any more, but that was because I never saw anyone. Dad had made the apprenticeship sound really exciting. I'd expected to be making deals, buying and selling stuff, but he did all that himself. I just used heavy lift and transport sleds to shift junk round the scrap yard, or to dump rubbish through the recycling machines. If Dad would...

My lookup played a couple of warning notes, and I braced myself for the sickening sound of the male singer that would come next. I'd found this lookup in a rubbish delivery a few days ago, one of the latest models in apparently perfect condition. I'd happily transferred all my personal stuff to it yesterday, before discovering exactly why its previous owner had thrown it away. It was suffering some sort of data corruption, so once any options were set you could never change them. That meant I couldn't change the call alert from Zen

Arrath singing about his eternal devotion to a girl called Diamond. I couldn't change the default screen display from a barely legal image of a semi-clad Zen Arrath. I couldn't even stop getting alerts from the Zen Arrath fan club every time the man sneezed.

The voice of Zen Arrath started singing. "My love for you is..."

I checked the lookup, and saw it wasn't a recorded message from the Zen Arrath fan club this time, but an incoming call from my dad. I didn't want to talk to him, but I had to accept the call to shut up Zen Arrath.

"Krath, I'm coming home," said my dad. "Meet me at the house right away!"

"What? Why?"

He lowered his voice to speak in a dramatic whisper. "We're making a special broadcast. The underground network has just sent out a priority relay alert!"

"Amaz!" I jumped to my feet. "What are we relaying?"

"It's not safe to discuss this on the call system," said my dad. "We have to get back to the house."

He ended the call, and I started jogging across the scrap yard to the side gate. As I reached it, I saw a huge, emerald green butterfly was flapping its way along the fence towards me. I stopped and watched warily as the evil thing flew past me.

I hated Asgard butterflies. On my first day on this world, literally three hours after walking through an interstellar portal and arriving in Asgard Off-world, I'd seen a crimson and gold butterfly. I'd thought it was totally amaz, reached out to touch it, and the nuking thing bit me! Within minutes, my whole hand swelled up and went bright red. I ended up in a medical centre, with some officious doctor treating me for an allergic reaction while lecturing me on the stupidity of not reading the safety warnings when I arrived on a new planet. Given I'd lived on nine other worlds with perfectly safe butterflies, I felt he was being unfair, but I'd kept well clear of butterflies ever since.

I saw my dad heading for the house. The butterfly was at a safe distance now, so I went through the gate and hurried to join him at the front door. We went inside, and started our standard lock-down procedure ready for the broadcast. Secure the door. Set the windows to black-out mode. Activate all the proximity alarms.

Finally, we dragged the huge couch in the living room to one side, opened the trap door, and went down to the secret room under the floor. Dad turned on the glows, and hurried over to the bank of equipment by the side wall, throwing the master switch to turn everything on.

"So what's happening?" I asked.

"No time to explain," said my dad. "We've got to spread the news fast before the Military throw a security crackdown over the whole thing. You'll hear all the details when I'm making the broadcast."

"But you said *I* could do the next broadcast!"

"You can't do this one because it's a priority relay alert. You'll have to do the next one instead."

I glared at him. "You're always doing this. You keep saying I can do a broadcast, but it never happens."

"I promise faithfully you'll make the next broadcast. Now get the vid bees out."

"You promised faithfully last time!" I got the small spherical vid bees out of their case, and activated them. "You promised the time before that as well. It's always the same. You make the announcement. I get stuck with controlling the vid bees."

"This isn't about personal glory," said my dad. "This is about spreading the truth. Telling humanity the things the big newzie channels are scared to say. Reporting the real stories behind all the lies of Parliament of Planets and the Military."

I sent the vid bees floating through the air to the far end of the room, and started them recording. "I don't see why I can't be the one spreading the truth for once."

Dad put on his mask, and took up his position in front of the big "*Truth Against Oppression*" sign painted on the wall. Personally, I thought it was a boring name for a subversive news channel. All the other ten news channels in our underground network had more exciting names than us, but Dad never listened to my suggestions for a new name. He never let me do a broadcast. He never...

"Wake up, Krath," said my dad. "Can't you see I'm ready to broadcast?"

I sighed and went over to the equipment bank. "Broadcast in three, two, one..." I hit the red button.

"This is *Truth Against Oppression*," said my dad. "The channel that brings you the real truth behind the lying official propaganda. This is a special broadcast in addition to our regular weekly news update. Remember to follow our channel to make sure you never miss these vital extra broadcasts with emergency breaking news."

I frowned. Only the viewers who already followed our channel would be seeing this, so reminding them to follow us was a bit silly.

"Today we're relaying an emergency news story from an underground news channel in Delta sector," said my dad. "They're reporting a Military failure that's been covered up for three decades. One of the worlds in Epsilon sector was cleared as safe by Planet First teams, and moved into Colony Ten phase. A thousand trusting colonists went there only to find that every one of their babies was born Handicapped, with an immune system that couldn't survive on any world but Earth."

I gaped at him in shock. I could see why the underground network had called for a priority relay alert on this story. The Military had really messed up. They'd be eager to throw a news blackout on this before the word spread.

"Worse still," continued my dad, "the Military still refused to admit their failure. In an act of criminal irresponsibility, they allowed the planet Miranda to continue and be opened for full colonization."

I wasn't just shocked now, I was utterly grazzed. This story was huge!

My dad flourished an arm dramatically. "The Military have kept their secret for three decades now. For three decades, every baby born on Miranda has had to be portalled to Earth to save its life. For three decades, the parents of Miranda have wept for their lost children. For three decades, the Military have forced these people to suffer in silence, and..."

There was a sudden shrieking sound. I stared up at the ceiling in bewilderment, then realized one of the proximity alarms was going off. My dad broke off his sentence, and slammed his hand on the black button that cut the alarm siren. He started speaking again in an even more dramatic voice.

"This is *Truth against Oppression*. We are being raided! We are being raided! Going silent running now!"

I was so busy staring at Dad, that I didn't remember to hit the red button to cut the broadcast until he pointed at it. We practiced raid response drill every month, so I automatically followed the routine after that, shutting down the vid bees and all the electrical equipment. My dad was opening the hidden door to the reinforced panic room now, waving at me to join him, so I ran across and we both squeezed inside.

It was when Dad was closing the door behind us, that his lookup bleeped the house interior alarm signal. I'd been counting on this being a false alarm until then, but if the interior alarm was going off then someone was inside our house. This was really happening. Armed Military were searching our house. I was either going to be shot, or locked up in some Military prison for the rest of my life.

Nuke this! My dad might be happy to die to spread the truth, but I wasn't!

My dad shut the door, so we were in total darkness. For a

couple of minutes, there was just the sound of our breathing, and then there was another sequence of bleeps from my dad's lookup. I bit my lip. That was the alarm warning us that someone had opened the trapdoor. The Military were in the secret broadcast room now, so there was only the panic room door between us and them.

This was so unfair. I was going to die, and I hadn't even got my chance at doing the broadcast!

There was silence for about five more minutes, and then Zen Arrath started singing from my lookup. I jumped nervously, banged my head on the low ceiling, and tapped frantically at my lookup. In my haste to shut up Zen Arrath, I accidentally answered the call, and a grim female voice spoke.

"Krath, I assume you're inside that absurd panic room with your father. He's blocking my calls, so can you tell him there's no point in hiding from me. I'm right outside the door, and I intend to stay here until he comes out and talks to me!"

I wasn't sure if I was relieved or even more scared than before. It wasn't armed Military in our broadcast room. It was my Aunt Galina!

My dad groaned, squeezed past me to the door, and opened it. Aunt Galina watched us with that frosty look of hers as we scrambled out into the broadcast room. Dad straightened his clothes, and gave her an angry look.

"Why did you break into my house, and how did you get past the security defences?"

"It's not your house," said Aunt Galina, "it's mine, and I used my front door security master code to get in."

"It may be technically your house," said Dad, "but I'm renting it from you. I have a legal right to privacy. You've no business marching in here without my permission!"

Aunt Galina gave him a withering look. "You would have a legal right to privacy if you actually paid me the rent you owe, which you don't. You prefer to spend your money making illegal alterations to my property for your ridiculous vid channel, *Truth Against Depression*."

"It's not *Truth Against Depression*, it's *Truth Against Oppression*," said Dad, "and it's not ridiculous. We're performing an essential public service, telling people the truth behind all the official lies. You've interrupted a critically important broadcast by marching in here. We must tell the whole of humanity about Miranda!"

"Who is Miranda?" asked Aunt Galina.

"Miranda isn't a person," said Dad. "It's a planet in Epsilon sector. The Military messed up choosing it as a colony world. There aren't any children there, because every baby is born a throwback ape!"

Aunt Galina looked even more disapproving. "I dislike hearing the Handicapped described in such disrespectful terms. They've simply been born with a faulty immune system."

"It makes no difference what we call them," said Dad. "They aren't going to hear us because they can't leave Earth. Anyway, it's not as if they're really human."

"The Handicapped are as human as we are," said Aunt Galina. "In fact, I'd argue they're far more human than you."

My dad glared at her. "That's..."

She swept on, drowning him out with her voice. "What you're telling me is that you're spreading yet another wild rumour. There are several highly respected vid channels who take risks to reveal genuine stories of true public interest. Your channel can't hope to have the respect and viewers that they do, until you start checking your facts before broadcasting them."

"This story isn't a wild rumour," said Dad.

She sighed. "So you've checked the details yourself this time?"

"Well... no. It's totally unreasonable to expect me to go to a planet in Epsilon sector myself."

She sighed again, and tapped at her lookup for a moment. "Totally unreasonable? You could portal to Asgard Off-world, go through an interstellar portal to Gamma Sector Inter-change 6, join a cross-sector block portal to Epsilon, and arrive in time for the once a day block portal to Miranda in... just under thirty-six hours' time."

"All that portalling would be expensive," said Dad, "and I can't spend three or four days going to Epsilon sector. I've got a business to run."

"But I thought this was a critically important story," said Aunt Galina. "Still, if going to Miranda is too much trouble, you could verify your facts in other ways. Why not look up the contact information for a few random people on Miranda, and call them?"

"I can't start calling complete strangers on Miranda," said Dad.

"Then just check the import and export information for Miranda." Aunt Galina tapped at her lookup. "Miranda is an agricultural world, exporting food as well as genetically modified corn for the vaccine industry. It imports all its manufactured goods, including a surprising number of baby clothes for a world with no children."

"Information is easily faked," said Dad. "The Military cover things up very thoroughly."

"Some of those baby clothes are made here on Asgard," said Aunt Galina. "You could spend half an hour visiting the manufacturing centre and establishing the facts, but you won't because the truth might spoil your exciting story."

"It's not like that," said Dad. "I have to..."

Aunt Galina waved an imperious hand. "Be quiet! I've wasted more than enough time on yet another hopeless attempt to teach you basic common sense. I'm really here to see Krath."

I'd been watching in total silence, waiting for a chance to sneak off and hide in my bedroom, but now I gave a startled yelp. "Me? Why me?"

She turned to look at me, studying me as if I was some

sort of beetle. "Krath, your father is an idiot. You appear to be an idiot too, but I'm aware that may not be entirely your fault. Your father chose to drag you between a dozen different worlds without the slightest consideration for the effect on your education."

"That's not true," said Dad. "It was only ten worlds, and it wasn't my fault we had to keep moving. I was a fugitive! The Military were hunting me!"

Aunt Galina glanced at him. "If the Military had ever had the slightest interest in you, they could have arrested you years ago. They could have located you any time they wanted. Every time you step through a portal, your genetic code is scanned for billing purposes, and Military Intelligence have full access to that information."

She turned back to me. "I intervened when you were 14, Krath, offering your father this house if he settled down here on Asgard. I thought this would give you the chance to attend school normally, but instead I find he's turned what was a beautiful field into a scrap yard, and taken you out of school to use you as unpaid labour."

"Krath's not unpaid labour," said Dad. "I may not actually be paying him any credits, but he's being rewarded by learning valuable skills as my apprentice."

Aunt Galina ignored him. "Krath, I feel it is my duty as your aunt to make one final attempt to remove you from your father's scrap yard, and salvage you as a human being. I'm offering to take you to live in my own home."

"Live with you?" I gulped.

"You will live in my home until next Year Day, Krath. You will spend every waking hour of every day studying history.On Year Day 2789, you will become 18 and legally adult. At that point, you'll leave my home and become a student on a residential course run by University Asgard."

I'd been busily picturing life with Aunt Galina, and shuddering with horror, but the mention of University Asgard caught my attention. "What? I'd be a proper student?"

"Yes," said Aunt Galina. "I am an exceptional history teacher. I've often said that I could teach an intelligent rabbit enough history to get them into a leading university, and this is my chance to prove it."

I frowned. "I'm not a..."

"It's out of the question," said Dad. "Krath doesn't want to be a history teacher like you."

Aunt Galina laughed. "I can't imagine Krath as a history teacher. I think he'd be far more suited to practical excavation work, but this is his decision, not ours. Do you wish to spend the rest of your life doing unpaid work for your father, Krath, or would you like to be in a class with other students of your own age?"

I hesitated before speaking. "I'm not sure. Going to school never worked out very well. The other kids didn't like me. They all had friends already, and they called me names. I wouldn't have minded a bit of teasing. Friendly teasing means you're part of the group, accepted as one of them, but this was meant to be really nasty."

For a second, I thought there was a hint of sympathy in Aunt Galina's face. "This time, Krath, everyone in the class will be just as new as you, and trying to make friends. You will be living, working, and studying together, and I assure you there will be no bullying. I have contacts at University Asgard, and can make sure that you're in a class with a lecturer who deals with such problems quickly and effectively."

I thought for a moment. Spending months with Aunt Galina would be a nightmare, but at the end of it... "There'd be girls in this class?"

"There would be girls," said Aunt Galina. "You'd need to learn some social skills before they were interested in you, but there would be girls."

I considered that. If there were girls...

Aunt Galina tapped at her lookup. "It might help if you scan this."

Zen Arrath started singing from my lookup. I hastily cut him off and checked what Aunt Galina had sent me. A boring history text, rambling on about primitive twentieth century vids. I looked up at Aunt Galina. "This is the sort of thing I'll be stuck reading all day?"

She smiled. "You haven't got to the end yet, have you?"

I groaned, looked down at my lookup, and skimmed on. At the end of the text, there were two images. The first one showed some men in weird, uncomfortable looking clothes. The second was a girl on a beach. I blinked. The girl was only wearing a couple of strips of cloth. You could see her legs, all the way up to her...

I made a choking noise. My Aunt Galina couldn't possibly have realized that image was included in the text. Or could she?

"Most worlds, with the obvious exception of those in Beta sector, have strict rules against showing legally private body areas," said Aunt Galina. "However, clothing etiquette has varied greatly through history. Images for school texts are carefully chosen to avoid offending the moral sensitivities of pupils, or more correctly, to avoid scandalizing their parents."

She paused. "Personally, however, I strongly disapprove of such censorship. I believe students of history need unrestricted access to images to achieve a full understanding of the cultures in different places and different periods of history. What do you think, Krath?"

I nodded eagerly. "I agree. You're totally right."

"So, would you like to accept my offer and start studying history?" asked Aunt Galina.

I looked down at the twentieth century girl on my lookup. "Yes, I would! Just give me ten minutes to pack!"

DELTA SECTOR 2788 - FIAN

Hercules, Delta Sector, June 2788.

"Fian, you're a disgrace to the entire Eklund family," said my father.

He said that at least twice a week, but I'd no idea why he was saying it right now. It was eight o'clock in the morning, so I was exactly on time for breakfast. I'd only just walked into the room, so I hadn't had time to do anything he thought stupid. I couldn't have said the wrong thing, because I hadn't said a word yet.

I glanced at my mother, but she gave a slight shake of her head to indicate she didn't know what the problem was either. I sat down at the table in wary silence. I hadn't seen my father since yesterday morning. Had he found out some of the things I'd been hiding from him? The fact I had a girlfriend. The Gamma sector vids I'd been watching. The history thing.

But no, it couldn't be anything nearly that bad. If it was, my father wouldn't just be calling me a disgrace, he'd be exploding with rage. He was probably leading into another round of complaints about my long hair. He preferred a brutally close-trimmed hairstyle himself, and hated the way my blond hair trailed round my shoulders. Which was, of course, the main reason I kept it that long. My father had forced me to do so many things I hated; my long hair was a gesture of defiance.

"A son of mine coming second in a school physics test!" my father said in tones of deepest disgust.

That explained everything. My physics teacher had been messaging my father about me. Again! I could at least argue my case on this one. Not that my father would listen, he never did, but... "I got 96 per cent in the test."

"That's a very good result." My mother pulled a sympathetic face at me.

"No it isn't," said my father. "Not when someone else got 97 per cent. Why can't you be more like your sister?"

I braced myself to endure yet another lecture about my wonderful older sister who'd got her physics degree before she was 20. She'd moved away from Hercules a year ago, to join a specialist group on another Deltan world and research multi particle wave expansions. I'd hoped my father would stop comparing me to her after that, but things had got worse instead of better. While she lived at home, there were inevitable clashes between her and my father that stopped him seeing her as utterly perfect, but now...

"I hope you're thoroughly ashamed of yourself," said my father. "A great-grandson of the brilliant Jorgen Eklund failing a simple school physics test!"

Oh no! It wasn't going to be the lecture about my sister. It was going to be the lecture about Jorgen Eklund, which was even worse. My father seemed to have the idea that I only had to study a little harder to turn myself into a copy of my great-grandfather. Well, I couldn't, and I didn't want to either!

"I blame it on your ridiculous interest in history," said my father. "A totally pointless subject. Humanity shouldn't waste time looking back at the past; it should be working for the future!"

I wanted to argue that it was vital humanity learned the lessons of history, because otherwise we'd keep repeating the same mistakes over and over again, but that would be an incredibly bad idea. It was four years since my father had told me to take an optional specialist technology course at school, and I'd signed up for a three month history module instead. When he found out what I'd done, my father had been furious and ordered me to drop the history module at once. I'd tried standing up to him, told him how much I hated physics, and said that I wanted to move from the science stream to the history stream.

That started an epic battle between us. I lost. My school wouldn't let me change from the science stream to the history stream without my parents' consent, and my mother sympathized with me but got shouted down by my father. Ever since then, I'd carefully avoided mentioning history, but my father still held a grudge over my brief rebellion, and kept blaming all my failures on it.

"I remember visiting my grandfather in his laboratory at University Hercules when I was only 10 years old," continued my father. "It was a true inspiration seeing everything that he'd achieved. I remember how he looked at me and said..."

I was 17 years old, and Father must have told me this story at least twenty times during every single one of those years. By now I could recite every word in my sleep. I tuned out my father's voice, and concentrated on eating a bowl of crunchy blue slices of my favourite Hercules melon. It was just the way I liked it, packed with the tiny juicy seeds that hovered on the borderline between sweet and sour. Some people liked the seedless varieties of Hercules melon, but I...

"Are you listening to me?" demanded my father.

"Yes, Father." I scraped the last stray melon seeds from my bowl. I'd definitely heard a mention of the Military. "Great-grandfather told you how the Military tried to sabotage his research by dumping him under planetary arrest here on Hercules when it was still just a frontier world. He didn't let that stop him though. He founded University Hercules and carried on his work anyway."

Father nodded, and continued the story. "Your great-grandfather left a shining legacy to human knowledge. The only ambition he never achieved was winning a Nobel, and that was because of a blatant injustice. His improvements to the design of the interstellar portals and their relay system totally revolutionized cross-sector portal travel, but the Nobel Committee back then deliberately overlooked him."

I felt the Nobel Committee had good reason to overlook my great-grandfather's work. Jorgen Eklund hadn't just used highly unethical research methods, he'd been rumoured to be involved in the Persephone incident, and there was absolutely no doubt that he'd started the planetary civil war on Freya in Alpha sector.

I opened my mouth to say that, but my mother gave me a pleading look, so I picked up my glass of frujit and sipped it instead.

"I wish you'd had the chance to meet him yourself," said my father.

I didn't. I was deeply grateful for the fact that Jorgen Eklund had reached his hundredth and died long before I was born. It was embarrassing enough having him as my great-grandfather when he was dead. I shuddered at the thought of what my life would be like if he was still alive. I hated the way everyone constantly talked to me about my sister, asking whether she'd published any more papers, but if my great-grandfather was still alive it would be far worse. I'd probably have people asking whether he'd started any more wars yet!

"On Year Day 2789, you'll be 18 and will start your physics degree at University Hercules," my father relentlessly carried on with his lecture. "That means you've only got six months to improve the standards of your work. You can't carry on in this slapdash way when my own colleagues are teaching you. Remember that I'll have been awarded my Nobel Prize by then, so I won't want to be embarrassed by hearing bad reports of my son."

Mother grabbed at the chance to interrupt his lecture. "Yes, the deadline for work to be considered for the Nobel is less than a week away now, and there really is nothing else significant in the Astrophysics area this year, so... It's wonderful to think that you'll finally have the recognition you deserve."

Father nodded. "Ever since I heard my grandfather talk about the one ambition he'd never achieved, this has been my dream. To make up for that old injustice, by winning a Nobel Prize myself. I'm planning to use my acceptance speech to dedicate the prize to my grandfather's memory."

I blinked. The Nobel ceremony would be held on Adonis in Alpha sector. I knew my father could be incredibly insensitive, but surely even he should realize that mentioning Jorgen Eklund's name on any planet in Alpha sector was a really bad idea.

My father stood up, his mind clearly focused on his Nobel now rather than on his failure of a son. "I'll make a few notes about my speech before going to the university."

He headed off to his study, and I turned to give my mother a worried look. "We can't let Father make an acceptance speech that's all about Jorgen Eklund. Not when he's on the capital planet of Alpha sector. He'll have the audience throwing things at him!"

She frowned. "I know your great-grandfather left Alpha sector under unfortunate circumstances."

"Unfortunate circumstances!" I repeated. "Mother, it was a lot more than unfortunate. He started a war on Freya!"

"That wasn't a war. It was merely a planetary incident. A conflict has to escalate beyond a single planet before it counts as a real war."

"That may be technically true, but I think the people who died on Freya felt it was a real war."

She sighed. "I suppose you're right, but hopefully everyone will have forgotten all about it by now. It was a very long time ago."

"Not long enough," I said grimly. "And it wasn't just the war; there was what happened on Persephone too. You can't tell me people have forgotten about that. The ent vid channels show almost as many horror vids about what happened on Persephone as they do about Thetis and Gymir. Given the number of people who died on Persephone, and the state of the survivors afterwards..."

"Your great-grandfather was never proved to be personally involved in the Persephone incident."

"He was proved to belong to the group that caused it. You have to talk sense into Father. Make him see he can't mention Jorgen Eklund in his acceptance speech."

Mother sighed again. "I'll do my best, but you know what your father's like." She checked the time on her lookup. "It's nearly half past eight. What day is it on your school timetable?"

My school worked on a complex 21 day timetable, which confused even the teachers. Everyone else complained about it, but I found it very useful. My father didn't even try to understand it, so he'd got no idea what I should be doing on any particular day.

"It's day 6 of the 21 day cycle," I said. "That's a rest day for the school science stream."

"Ah," said my mother. "You'll be... *resting* then."

I nodded. "I'll be... *resting.*"

I went over to a cupboard, collected a couple of cartons of food and drink, and then tiptoed through the hall. My father's study door was closed, so I made it outside without any more lectures. I looked round warily at the luxury, one-storey homes. There was no one outside the houses, and the central garden with the local portal in the middle seemed totally deserted.

I walked across to the portal, gave a last paranoid look over my shoulder just in case my father had materialized out of the ground behind me, and dialled my school. The second the portal established, I stepped through, arriving on the

expanse of bare concraz in front of the array of school buildings. No one else should be portalling in for at least another
fifteen minutes, but I still sprinted madly to the small building
at the far end, entered the code into the lock plate, went
inside, and shut the door behind me.

Now I was safe. The cross-sector education laws said that
every school had to have sports facilities and offer sport as a
voluntary option for its pupils. Since Delta sector was science
obsessed in general, and Hercules was the most science
obsessed of all its two hundred and two planets, my school
only went through the motions of complying with those laws.
This small, empty dome, and the area of grass beside it, were
the school sports facilities. Sport was listed as a voluntary
optional course, but there was no sports teacher, and no
pupils ever signed up to do it. That meant nobody except me
and my two friends had entered this dome in the last four
years.

I went across to the table and three chairs that my friends
and I had "borrowed" from another classroom, sat down, put
the cartons of food under the table to eat later, and took out
my lookup. I checked for messages, and saw my last physics
homework had been returned with the highest possible mark.
I didn't bother looking at my teacher's comments. Even
though I'd got a perfect mark, he was bound to have said
something about how my sister would have done better.

My life would be a lot easier if my physics teacher hadn't
taught my older sister. My life would be a lot easier if my
sister had gone to a different school. In fact, I sometimes felt
my life would be a lot easier if I'd never had a sister at all!

But even if my sister had never existed, I'd still have
suffered from being compared to the rest of my depressingly
brilliant relatives. My father, my mother, my uncles, my
cousins, my grandparents, and of course my notorious great-
grandfather were all genius level scientists as well, while I was

just reasonably clever. Short of annihilating my entire family tree, both living and dead, there was no way of changing the fact I was the Eklund family failure.

I briefly, and pointlessly, wished I'd been born to different parents, perfectly average and very boring parents, who had ordinary expectations of their son. Parents who'd have been pleased and proud of me for coming second in a school physics test.

I was being unfair to my mother though. I knew she was disappointed in me, she was bound to be in the circumstances, but she did her best to hide it.

I sighed, put my lookup in my pocket, went across to the loose section of dome floor, lifted it up, and took out my secret second lookup. This was a very basic model, but it had one huge advantage over the advanced one that my father had given me. He couldn't run remote checks to watch what I was doing on it, because he didn't know it existed.

I heard the door open behind me, took a fast look over my shoulder, and saw both my friends had arrived together. They shut the door carefully behind them, and Macall spread his arms in an expansive gesture.

"Tremble, oppressed ones of Delta sector. The corrupting influence of Gamma sector is among you!"

Valin hit him, and turned to eagerly look at me. "How was last night's date with your girlfriend? Did you get anywhere?"

I retrieved both their secret lookups from under the floor and handed them over, before putting the floor back into place, standing up, and answering the question. "I got my face slapped, called a sexual pervert, and dumped!"

"Oh." Valin slumped down into one of the chairs. "Things didn't go too well then."

"Sexual pervert!" Macall repeated. "What the chaos did you do to the girl?"

"I tried to hold her hand," I said. "I thought she wanted me to push the boundaries a bit, but apparently I'd misread the signals."

"All that for trying to hold her hand?" Macall gave a sad shake of his head.

"No respectable Deltan girl would dream of holding hands with a boy without a Twoing contract." I mimicked my ex-girlfriend's voice as I quoted her.

I sat down at the table, dropped my secret lookup on top of it, and stared down at it gloomily. "It's not as if I'd have objected to having a Twoing contract. My father would throw a fit, saying I shouldn't let emotions distract me from my studies, but I'd have stood up to him over it. I just wanted a little reassurance first."

Macall laughed. "A little reassurance that you wouldn't fight a huge battle with your father, and commit yourself to a legal contract for months, then discover you were Twoing with a complete frost of a girl?"

"Well, yes," I admitted. "It's so difficult to tell if a girl is freezing you off to obey Deltan social conventions, or if she really is a human icicle."

Macall sat down in the third chair. "It's been five years since my parents dragged me to Hercules to further their wretched careers, but I still don't believe how prudish things are here. It's so unfair. If I was back on Asgard in Gamma sector, dating a girl there..."

There was several minutes' silence, while all three of us daydreamed about dating a girl in Gamma sector. Macall had left Gamma sector when he was 12, so he'd never actually dated anyone there himself, but he'd seen his older brother kissing a girlfriend. Valin and I were basing our ideas on the Gamma sector vids we'd seen.

Normally you had to be 18 or have parental permission to watch Gamma sector vids, but Macall had dual Deltan and Gamman citizenship, so he had free access. He let me and Valin watch his vids with him. My personal favourite was a series called *Stalea of the Jungle*.

"I wish I was Stalea's boyfriend," I said.

"But she lives in a jungle village on a world that's been cut off from civilization," said Macall. "That vid series has a totally ridiculous plot."

"It's not that ridiculous," said Valin. "Civilization virtually collapsed after Exodus century. A lot of worlds had their interstellar portals fail in the early part of the twenty-fifth century and genuinely were totally isolated."

"What about the jungle though?" asked Macall. "The Military wouldn't open up a new world for colonization with a proposed inhabited continent covered in jungle. Especially a jungle with monsters in it."

"I don't care about the plot being unrealistic," I said. "I like the way Stalea throws her boyfriend across a jungle clearing, leaps on him, and forcibly kisses him. If only my girl-friend, I mean my *ex*-girlfriend, was like that."

"You'd need more than a Twoing contract to get a Deltan girl to kiss you like that," said Macall. "I don't think even mar-riage would be enough. Anyway, being thrown across a jungle clearing could be extremely painful if you landed on a rock."

"Stalea's boyfriend never lands on rocks," said Valin, in a dreamy voice. "She always throws him somewhere soft, and the way she kisses him is totally amaz. It's a pity the credits start rolling as soon as it gets really interesting."

Macall shook his head in mock disapproval. "I'm shocked! Well behaved 17-year-old Deltan boys shouldn't be having impure thoughts about girls kissing them."

"I'm a very badly behaved Deltan boy," I said. "Just ask my father and he'll tell you! Anyway, the thing I like best about Stalea is that she makes it perfectly clear what she wants from her boyfriend. If my ex-girlfriend had made her rules clear to start with, then we might still be together."

I paused and sighed. "Maybe it's a good thing my girlfriend dumped me. Being involved with a girl would make things even more difficult. I couldn't leave Hercules if I was in a relationship, not unless she'd leave with me, and..."

"Forget the girlfriend!" said Macall. "We have work to do. We're supposed to be reading up on the expansionists winning the key vote in 2370."

We all turned on our secret lookups, and there was total silence while we read the recommended history text on how the expansionist victory meant the Military could continue opening up the Beta sector planets for colonization. Personally, I felt the historian who'd written it was far too positive about the expansionist victory being a good thing. The greedy colonization of more and more worlds had led to the near total collapse of civilization and the loss of huge amounts of human knowledge. Vast swathes of historical knowledge, culture and...

A bell rang loudly overhead, telling us the first school class of the day was starting. The three of us shut down our lookups, waited exactly five minutes, then cautiously peered out of the door. There was no one in sight, so we sprinted for the dome next door, skidding in through the open doorway, and pausing to close the door behind us.

"Welcome," said the history teacher, Larsson. "As I was saying, I've now got your first round of examination results."

The four legal members of the history class were sitting at the front desks. They were all boys, of course. Schools on Hercules all accepted both boys and girls, but even the tiniest classes were strictly segregated.

Macall, Valin, and I sat down. We had the three desks closest to the big display board, so if any outsiders walked into the class, we could hide behind it. That had only happened three times in the last four years. History, literature, and art classes were always timetabled on science rest days, when there were just a handful of teachers and students at the school.

Once we'd sat down, Larsson continued. "You'll be glad to hear that you've all got the top grade. It's a shame I can only put four of you on the official school results list. If I put all seven of you down, then that would put this school at the top of the Hercules history results table for this year."

He paused. "Now, although I deeply admire the determined way our three gatecrashers have given up their free time to stick with their history studies over the last four years, we're reaching the real crisis point. The Cross-sector University Application Process opened today for all courses starting immediately after Year Day 2789. I could quietly add names to a history examination entry list without anyone noticing, but university applications are a very different matter."

He pulled a face. "I'll happily assist any of you wishing to apply to do a Pre-history Foundation course but, given the way your parents blocked you moving from the school science stream to the school history stream, I assume you'll meet strong opposition at home."

Macall nodded. "We've got a plan to deal with that. We'll start by doing what our parents expect, putting in applications to University Hercules to study physics. We can change those applications at any time until the application process closes. We wait until the last day, and then change them to..."

All three of us chorused it in unison. "Pre-history Foundation course at University Asgard in Gamma sector!"

"I hope you realize that you won't actually do the course on Asgard," said the teacher. "All Pre-history Foundation courses are held on Earth. You'll be learning about the days when humanity only lived on Earth, and studying the ruins of the ancient cities."

"We understand that," I said. The course would be run by University Asgard under Gamma sector rules, but the classes would take place on Earth, the home world of humanity. I'd be seeing the places where the ancient civilizations had flourished, walking in the steps of the famous people of pre-history. It was going to be utterly perfect, totally zan, all my dreams coming true at once!

Larsson shook his head. "All right, we'll have everything ready so you can make your changes quickly, and swap your physics teacher's supporting statements for mine, but you'd better think through exactly how your parents will react when they find out what you've done."

"Maybe they won't be that annoyed," said Valin.

"They won't be annoyed," said Macall. "They'll be incandescent with rage, but what can they do to stop us? By the time they find out, the Cross-sector University Application Process will have closed, so they won't be able to change anything."

"That's true for you, Macall," said Larsson, "and for Valin too, because your parents are ordinary school teachers. Fian's in a very different situation though. His father doesn't just work in the Physics Department of University Hercules, he runs it, and may be able to persuade his colleagues to accept a late application."

"My father could definitely persuade them," I said. "Everyone in the Physics Department is terrified of him, but he can't change my course application without my agreement. I just have to stay firm for two weeks until the course places are allocated."

"I wish you the best of luck with that, because it won't be easy," said Larsson. "After the incident when you took a history module, I had the dubious pleasure of meeting your father, so I know exactly what you're up against."

I knew it would be far from easy, but I was counting on one thing to help me. The Cross-sector Nobel Committee formally announced its decision in October, and the awards ceremony was at the start of December. My father would find out about my university application in the ecstatic period between being officially announced as the Nobel Prize winner and actually holding the award. It was over optimistic to think that he wouldn't care what I was doing, but he should be too occupied with accepting the congratulations of all his colleagues, and gloating over fulfilling his lifelong ambition, to spend much time shouting at me.

Larsson dropped the subject of university applications after that, and started us debating the set text we'd been reading. I argued the case that the expansionist victory was a disaster, while Macall claimed it was a good thing. Earth had already been strained too much by founding all the colony worlds of Alpha sector, and would have collapsed anyway.

"Yes, but..." I broke off my sentence because my lookup was chiming for an emergency call. I grabbed it, checked the caller, and saw it was my mother. She wouldn't call me on my secret lookup unless something was desperately wrong.

"Sorry," I said, "I really must answer this."

I hurried outside, sprinted back to the safety of the sports dome, and answered the call.

My mother looked apologetically at me. "I'm sorry to call you like this, but I had to warn you..." She seemed to be looking past me, checking what she could see of my surroundings. "Nobody can hear us, can they?"

"No," I said. "I'm totally alone."

Despite my words, she lowered her voice to a barely audible whisper. "It's your father. A friend on the Cross-sector Nobel Committee has called him with some unfortunate news."

I stared at her. "You don't mean...?"

She nodded. "Two researchers at University Mextli have announced an incredible breakthrough."

"But... It's surely too late for their research to be considered for this year's Nobel. Nothing is eligible unless it's independently verified and replicated by other researchers before the deadline, and that's only days away."

"Apparently it's already been verified," my mother interrupted me.

"What? But if that's true, why didn't Father know about it?"

"This was a joint civilian and Military research project, so the results were classified. The findings were given to two other University research groups to verify, but they had to keep them secret as well. Nobody else knew anything about it until yesterday, when the Military cleared everything for publication."

"Oh." I was silent as I thought this through. "Is there any chance at all of the Nobel?"

Mother shook her head. "Viewed dispassionately, your father's work is solid, thorough, but not exactly innovative."

My mother wasn't just my father's wife, but one of his research assistants, and his staunchest supporter. If she admitted that my father's work was solid, but the rival research was an incredible breakthrough, then all hope of a Nobel had gone up in smoke. My father and I did nothing but argue, but I still had to feel sorry for him.

"This is obviously going to be a huge disappointment for Father," I said.

"And a major embarrassment too," said Mother. "Everyone was assuming he'd get the Nobel. All the staff at University Hercules were counting on it boosting the prestige of not just the Physics Department but the whole university, and your father..."

She hesitated for a moment. "Your father's made a few premature remarks about getting the Nobel this year. There are one or two people with reason to dislike him, and they may take the opportunity to make his life difficult."

I groaned. I knew Mother was politely understating the situation. The truth was that my father had been making cutting remarks about other people's research for years. By now, there weren't just one or two people who disliked him, but a whole host of people who really hated him.

"You mean that Father's been going round boasting about how he'll get the Astrophysics Nobel this year, so his enemies are going to make the most of his disappointment?"

She nodded. "The next six months are going to be a very difficult time for him. We'll have to be prepared for him to be... a little impatient sometimes. I realize that's likely to complicate your plans."

I groaned again. I'd thought it was good that my father would find out about my university application in the period between the announcement of the Nobel winners and the awards ceremony, but if his coveted Astrophysics Nobel was going to other researchers, particularly ones involved with the Military, then...

"Are you sure you still want to apply to do history at University Asgard?" asked my mother.

"Not history, Mother, pre-history," I automatically corrected her. "The Foundation course focuses on the period of history before interstellar portal travel, which is called pre-history."

She waved a hand, indicating that she didn't think there was much difference. "Pre-history then. I thought your girlfriend was planning to study physics here at University Hercules. Surely that changes things?"

I shook my head. "Not really. My girlfriend dumped me last night."

"Ah." My mother sighed. "So you're positive this is what you want to do?"

I couldn't bear to go and study physics at University Hercules, with the shadow of the brilliant Jorgen Eklund looming over me, and my father constantly watching me and calling me a failure. I was going to study the pre-history I loved on the world where those events had actually happened. I was going to be in a class where no one knew or cared about my brilliant family, and people wouldn't judge me against impossible standards. Maybe I'd even meet a Gamman girl who wouldn't dump me for trying to hold her hand.

"I'm positive."

"At first I thought your interest in history wouldn't last, but given you've put in so much work over the last four years..." Mother paused. "I accept you're old enough to make your own decisions, and you've a perfect right to live the life you want. I'll support you in this, but your father..."

I nodded. "I know. When Father finds out about this, he's going to be furious. Things were bad four years ago, but this time will be far, far worse. I'm not going to give in though. Four years ago, Father could force his decision on me, but this time he can't. This time I'm going to win!"

EPSILON SECTOR 2788 - AMALIE

Miranda, Epsilon Sector, June 2788.

I was going to the afternoon school shift, so I didn't need to get there until one o'clock, but I was still going to be late. Partly because I'd been babysitting my three youngest brothers and sisters all morning, partly because the water pipe from the spring needed unblocking for the third time this week, and partly because I'd heard the chickens squawking for help and had to go and rescue them from a moon monkey that was peering nosily into the chicken run. Moon monkeys were one of the original native species of Miranda, perfectly harmless herbivores, but our chickens were terrified of their round, glowing faces.

These things were all just excuses, of course. The real reason I'd set off late for school was because I knew exactly what would happen when I got there. In fact, it started before I was anywhere near the school, because Torrin Summerhaze was lying in wait for me at the portal that was shared between the dozen nearest farms.

It would take me an hour to walk to the next nearest portal, so I gritted my teeth and marched up to this one, pointedly avoiding eye contact with Torrin. That didn't stop him happily jeering at me.

"Old maid! Old maid! Amalie is the old maid!"

I didn't turn to look at him, just reached out with my right hand to slap him on the back of the head.

"Ow!" he complained. "That hurt."

"It was meant to hurt."

I reached out to set the destination for the portal, but hesitated at the last moment. It was one of the economy models, just offering the six most important local destinations: Jain's Ford Settlement Central, Jain's Ford School, Mojay's General Store, the livestock market, the vet, and the medical centre over at Falling Rock Settlement.

If you wanted to go anywhere else, you had to portal to Settlement Central first. That had a proper portal you could use to travel anywhere on the inhabited continent of Miranda, though naturally the portalling charges were a lot higher. The only time I'd been through it was last year, when my parents took all eleven of us to visit Memorial. We'd seen the sea, and the hilltop monument marking where the Military handed Miranda over to the first colonists thirty-one years ago. It was a totally zan day, apart from the twins falling in a rock pool so they stank of seaweed.

Right now, I felt like going to Settlement Central and portalling to Memorial again, or even all the way to Northern Reach. I'd seen images of the great cliffs there on the Miranda Rolling News channel. I could see those cliffs for myself, and have a glorious day of freedom, far away from Jain's Ford Settlement, Jain's Ford School, and people like Torrin Summerhaze. The snag was that I'd have to come back and face them all at the end of it. I'd have spent credits I couldn't afford, and it would change nothing.

I set the destination to the school, and walked through the second the portal established. I stepped out of the portal in the school field, and headed for the nearest of the six grey flexiplas domes, the one that was labelled with a large white number 6 and a lopsided pink hummingbird.

The number 6 was the official school dome label. The pink

hummingbird was a legacy of when the boys in the year above us got drunk on their last day at school and found a stray can of paint. Rodrish Jain had climbed onto the dome roof to finish painting the hummingbird's wings, stopped in the middle to shout and wave at the rest of us, fell off, and was portalled to the medical centre at Falling Rock with a broken arm. There was a rumour that Doc Jumi had fixed Rodrish's arm, and then locked him in quarantine for twenty-four hours in case his pink spots were a sign of a previously undiscovered Mirandan disease. It was probably true. Doc Jumi had an evil sense of humour.

Torrin came through the portal and chased after me. "Amalie, I could help you solve your problem. Marry me!"

I stopped walking, looked him up and down, shook my head sadly, and gave him the standard frontier planet rejection line. "Come back when you've got a farm!"

He sighed, and trailed along after me to dome 6. As we went inside, twenty boys looked at me, stood up, and yelled it in unison. "Old maid! Old maid! Amalie is the old maid!"

Last year, there'd been twenty-one boys and eighteen girls in our class. Here on Miranda, as on most of the planets in Epsilon sector, you could have Twoing contracts at 16 and marry at 17. On Year Day 2788, we'd all turned 17, and seven of the girls instantly proved themselves perfect frontier world women by having Year Day weddings. Admittedly, in Rina's case, there was a scandal over her last minute change of husband.

Norris was still fuming about that, and you could hardly blame him. He'd been Twoing with Rina for ten months, so when she dumped him in the middle of their wedding and married another man it was a shock for everyone. The fact the other man was Norris's older brother, made things even worse. Jain's Ford Settlement was pretty equally divided between those who thought Rina had done the right thing, those who thought she should have stuck with Norris, and those who thought she should have married both of them. I was the exception. I thought it would have been much more sensible for Rina to cancel the wedding, and think things over for a few weeks before she married anyone, but it was her life, not mine.

Over the next three months, nine of the other girls had got married as well, though without any more scandals. My friend, Cella, had held out for a further two months before caving into social pressure and marrying yesterday. Now there were twenty-one boys, seventeen empty desks, and me. I was the class old maid. Worse than that, I was the settlement old maid, because all the girls my age who'd left school at 15 were married as well.

Teacher Lomas let the boys enjoy their fun for a minute, before yelling at them. "Quiet!"

They reluctantly calmed down, and Lomas turned to Torrin. "Why are you late? No, don't bother answering that. We can all guess the reason. We can all guess Amalie's answer too."

"Come back when you've got a farm," yelled the mob.

Torrin blushed.

"Time for work now," said Lomas.

I sat down at my desk, took out my lookup, turned it on, and frowned as I saw the display flicker wildly for a moment or two before focusing properly. My lookup had started doing this a couple of months ago, and it seemed to be getting worse. I hoped like chaos that it wasn't going to break down entirely. I was the third eldest of eleven children. Schooling on Miranda was free, and my parents believed in education, but it was a struggle for them to afford the vital lookups we all needed to scan the school texts and send and receive work assignments. A girl of my age had no real need to be in school, so if my lookup broke down...

"We're revising Farming Ecology today," said Lomas, "starting with methods of limiting potentially harmful interactions between imported Earth and native Mirandan species."

There was a chorus of groans, and one of the boys in the front row mimed strangling himself before collapsing on his desk.

Lomas sighed. "Year End is six months away now, and the school will be closed for a month during harvest. Those of you capable of subtracting one from six can work out you have barely five months of study time left before you leave school. You must pass all the modules of your Farming Studies Certificate before then, or you can't register to do community service and earn yourselves a farm."

"The others need to do community service to earn farms," said Palmer Nott smugly, "but I don't. I've already got a farm, because my father bought me one yesterday. We'll be ordering my machinery next month."

There was dead silence as every other boy in the room looked at him in shock, which rapidly changed to bitter resentment. Palmer was deeply unpopular in the class. That wasn't because he was an incomer from Loki in Gamma sector, rather than born on this planet. Miranda had only opened for full colonization twenty-one years ago, so most of the class were incomers. Palmer's unpopularity was because he constantly rubbed everyone's nose in the fact his father was sickeningly wealthy. Since he arrived two years ago, we'd all had to suffer him showing off his expensive clothes that were totally unsuitable for farm work, and his fancy lookup with all the special features, but this...

All the other boys would have to do three years of community service to earn their farms. That was what my two older brothers were doing right now, patiently working to prepare farmland and build houses for others, waiting for the day that the next farm and house would be for them.

Palmer wouldn't have to do that though. His father had just handed him a farm, and his easy ride wasn't stopping there. All parents did their best to give their sons starting seed and livestock, especially the vital pair of horses, but Palmer's father was buying him machinery too. No endless hours of backbreaking labour for Palmer. He was going to stand idly by, watching while his fields were ploughed by machines. Given how much I resented that on behalf of my brothers, chaos knew how the boys around me were feeling.

"Obviously I can't start running the farm until I'm 18," said Palmer, "but my father said it was best to buy me one now to make sure I get prime land by the river, and order the machinery early because there's a waiting list for the next bulk shipment from Gamma sector."

He turned to grin at me. "Amalie, I know girls don't count marriage proposals from men without farms, but you'll have to consider mine!"

If he'd been within arm's reach, I'd have hit him. He wasn't, so I gave him a withering look of contempt. "Come back when you're a human being, Palmer."

"Yaya! Yaya! Yaya!" All the boys in the room were shouting their approval of my words, hammering on their desks with their fists.

Lomas pointedly put his hands over his ears, waited until the noise started to flag, and then yelled at them. "Shut up!"

The shouting and hammering gradually petered out, and Lomas turned to Palmer. "Go home!"

"What?" asked Palmer.

"Go home!" repeated Lomas. "If you stay here and keep talking about your prime farmland, and ordering your machinery early to avoid the waiting list, someone is going to punch you. Quite possibly me."

Palmer hesitated, and then stood up. "I don't understand why you're all acting like this. Rodrish Jain was in the year above us. Nobody minded when his father gave him a farm. In fact, the whole school cheered for him."

Everyone had been angry already, but now we were furious. Torrin was the fastest shouting a reply.

"Your answer's in our settlement name, idiot! This is Jain's Ford. It's called that because Rodrish Jain's parents led the first colonists here when the Military cleared Miranda to enter Colony Ten phase. Those colonists came when there was nothing but a heap of supplies and flexiplas panels. They had to clear the farms. They had to build the houses. Most of all they had to live here for ten years in quarantine to prove the Military hadn't missed anything dangerous, and that Miranda was safe for humans. If there weren't just the usual problems between imported and native species, but something utterly lethal, those first colonists would have died!"

Torrin paused for a second to breathe before ranting on in an impassioned voice. "That's why we honour the Founding Families, that's why they were rewarded with land grants, and that's why everyone cheered for Rodrish. Your father's rich, Palmer, so you jumped ahead of us in the queue and took prime farm land from under our noses. Rodrish wasn't queue jumping, his father owned that land at Jain's Ford before any of our parents set foot on Miranda. Rodrish wasn't taking anything from us; his father gave us our world!"

"Yaya! Yaya! Yaya!" The other boys shouted their approval again.

Lomas lifted a hand to stop them. "Go home, Palmer, and don't come back for a week. You're suspended."

"You can't suspend me," said Palmer. "I didn't break any rules. My father will complain to the school board. You could lose your job!"

"Watch me cower in fear," said Lomas, in his most sarcastic voice. "Since Teacher Horath moved to the school at the new Twin River Settlement, I'm the only teacher in this school qualified to either teach or assess students working on their Farming Studies Certificate. I teach the 16-year-olds in first shift school from eight in the morning to one in the afternoon. I teach the 17-year-olds in second shift school from one in the afternoon to six in the evening. Four nights a week, I teach evening classes for all the boys who left school at 15 to work on their parents' farms."

He pulled a face. "I'm doing all that solo because the school board have been trying and failing to recruit another qualified teacher for the last fifteen months. If they fired me today, I could get a new job tomorrow, but everyone studying for their Farming Studies Certificate would have to join waiting lists for places at other schools, and given schools always give priority to students from their own settlement..."

He paused. "For the final time, go home, Palmer. You've been living on this planet for two years now, and you still don't seem to understand the basics about a frontier world. You can't buy respect with credits. You have to earn it yourself. Go home and think about that, before your classmates take you outside and beat the lesson into you."

Palmer finally turned and left the dome. Lomas watched the door shut and then started talking again. "There are currently over two hundred known potentially harmful interactions between imported Earth and native Mirandan species. The following farming procedures must be enforced to prevent these interactions. Firstly, apple trees can only be grown within secure caging since their juice is toxic to..."

I stopped listening, because I'd completed all my Farming Studies Certificate modules four months ago. Most of the girls in the class hadn't bothered doing the final assessments, since having the actual certificate wasn't relevant for a girl, but my mother said that a farmer's wife needed to know these things to be able to help her husband.

Once I'd finished all the Farming Studies modules, Lomas had started sending me other texts to keep me busy. To begin with, they'd been on random subjects, but lately they'd mostly been about history. The latest one was about how the near collapse of civilization back in 2409 had left many worlds totally isolated when their interstellar portals failed.

I dutifully started scanning the text, but it was hard to concentrate on the problems of humanity several centuries ago when I had my own problems right now. Ever since I was 16, family, neighbours and friends had all been busily asking me what man I favoured. When I turned 17 last Year Day, the pressure had increased, with them actively suggesting husbands to me, or even pointedly reminding me of my duty to marry.

Chaos, I knew it was my duty to marry. Miranda was a frontier world with exactly the same problem all frontier worlds had. Too many men. You needed a lot of people to build a new world, and there were always more male than female colonists arriving. Some men were happy to marry other men, but most wanted wives. It was a frontier girl's duty to help solve that problem by marrying quickly, preferably to two men rather than just one, and having a lot of children, preferably daughters.

My parents had been patient at first, but three months ago they'd anxiously asked whether I had a problem about getting married. I couldn't tell the full truth, which was that I didn't have a problem about getting married, but I did have a problem about having children. As the eldest daughter in a family of eleven children, I seemed to have spent my entire childhood helping my mother change nappies and feed babies. Three of the Year Day brides had already proudly announced they were expecting babies. If I married now, then I'd probably be changing my own baby's nappies within a year.

I didn't want to go straight from caring for baby brothers and sisters to caring for my own baby. Saying that would sound like I was complaining, or criticizing my mother, and I wasn't. Sons were expected to help their father with the farm work. Daughters were expected to help their mother with the babies. That was the frontier life. My parents had been generous, making sacrifices to let us stay on at school when most children had to leave at 15, and I was deeply grateful to them.

In the end, I just said that I didn't want to rush such an important decision. My parents had accepted that, scolding my brothers and sisters when they made jokes about me, and saying I was sensible to take my time to make the right choice. A month later though, they started getting restless again, and my mother gave me a long lecture about being too choosy. She said that no man was perfect – even my father had had a few bad habits he'd needed to break when she married him – and it was silly to spend too long watching other girls marry the best men so I was left to pick from the rejects.

Since then, every time one of my friends got married, the nagging voices around me had got louder and more persistent. Now I was the last unmarried 17-year-old girl in my settlement, the old maid of Jain's Ford, there'd be no respite at all.

I was going to have to marry someone, and it wasn't as if I was short of options. What Palmer had said was right, girls didn't count proposals from men who didn't have farms, but I'd had plenty of offers from those who did. If I ignored the ones who'd been drunk at the time, were over 30, or had dubious reputations...

I made a list of names on my lookup, counted them up, and made it nineteen respectable offers. Nineteen men, or pairs of men, who'd make perfectly good husbands. Marrying two men had obvious advantages, because their two separate farms could be combined or traded to make one large one. If I was going to marry two men, I felt it was simplest to marry brothers.

"Amalie."

I looked up, startled, and saw Lomas standing next to my desk.

"While the boys are working on their assignment, I thought we could have a private chat outside."

Lomas turned and headed for the door. I frowned, stood up, and followed him out of the dome, aware of the boys giving us curious looks. What was going on here? Lomas had never taken me out of the class before, and mentioning he wanted a private chat...

I blinked as the obvious answer occurred to me. Lomas

was unmarried, so he was going to make me an offer. That was a disconcerting idea. Slapping down the boys in my class was easy, but refusing an offer from my teacher would be embarrassing for both of us.

Lomas sat on the bench outside, and gestured at the space next to him. I sat down, keeping a careful gap between us. I daren't look at Lomas, so I faced straight forward, focusing on the mauve flowers of a field of Mirandan medcorn, our main cash crop for the vaccine industry. Now I was starting to get over the shock, I realized Lomas might have advantages as a husband. The main one being that because he'd been my teacher, Epsilon law said he couldn't marry me until a year after I'd left school.

If I agreed to marry Lomas, then even if I left school today, I'd have a whole year before the wedding. A whole year when no one would call me old maid, or criticize me for not doing my duty, because I was going to marry Lomas, a man who everyone in the settlement, with the possible exception of Palmer and his father, respected.

"Amalie," said Lomas, "I've been watching you with great interest for the last few months. As far as I know, you haven't accepted any marriage offer, though I'm sure you've had plenty. Is there an arrangement that you're keeping quiet for some reason? Perhaps there's a man you like, but he hasn't got his farm yet."

I liked the way Lomas was doing this. Checking his offer would be welcomed before he made it. Making sure he wouldn't put us both in a difficult situation. It showed he was a considerate man, and, looking at things practically, a teacher was a good match. It was one of the few jobs on Miranda that was paid solely in credits instead of bartered goods. Lomas might be a fraction over 30, but not much, so...

I took a deep breath and said the words that would reassure him that I was ready to hear his offer. "There's no arrangement."

"In that case..." He paused for a second. "Amalie, I'm a member of the Planetary Development Board Education Subcommittee."

Those weren't exactly the words I was expecting him to say. I turned to give him a bewildered look.

"Epsilon isn't the newest sector any longer," he continued. "The first Kappa sector worlds are coming out of Colony Ten phase and opening for full colonization. It's time for the worlds of Epsilon sector to start thinking beyond things like basic farming. A century from now, we want Epsilon to be a proud, established, self-sufficient sector, the way Delta sector is now. That isn't going to happen unless we start solving some major issues. What's the biggest problem that Miranda has right now?"

I just stared at him. It was clear now that Lomas wasn't making me an offer, so I'd absolutely no idea why we were having this conversation.

He sighed. "Think, Amalie. Remember all the things I said to Palmer about what would happen if the school fired me."

"Oh. Miranda doesn't have enough teachers."

Lomas nodded. "Not enough teachers. Not enough doctors. Not enough skilled people of any type. Not many of them come to the frontier as colonists, so every world in Epsilon sector has the same problem. It's crippling Epsilon's efforts to educate our next generation and to build a proper infrastructure for our worlds. The only way forward is to train our own teachers and doctors."

He paused. "The first few worlds colonized in Epsilon sector are all arguing about which gets to be the permanent capital planet. Miranda is one of the newer worlds, so they consider us insignificant, but the Planetary Development Board don't intend things to remain that way. We've been studying what happened in Delta sector. No one expected Isis to become the capital planet of Delta sector. No one expected Hercules to have the huge influence that it does. They became the most important worlds in Delta sector because they were the first to have true universities and train their own skilled people."

"I understand," I said, still not understanding anything at all.

"Miranda is going to follow their example," said Lomas. "Our planetary development plan involves concentrating a lot of our resources on founding University Miranda in four years' time, so we have one of the first universities in Epsilon sector. Building a university isn't a problem, but staffing it is. We hope to attract a few lecturers from the older sectors, but we also want some lecturers who were born here on Miranda. Their job won't just be to teach students, but to be role models, showing the young people of Miranda that they can aspire to more than farming."

He finally turned to face me. "We'd especially like the Miranda-born lecturers to include some women. I believe you could be one of those women, Amalie."

I blinked. "Me? But... How could I? You need qualifications to be a lecturer."

"Obviously you'd need to get your degree first, which will involve you going to a university in another sector."

I ran my fingers through my hair. Leave Miranda, leave Epsilon, leave all my family and friends to go to another sector! That was...

For a second, I imagined myself travelling to a world in one of the established sectors, seeing the sort of amaz places I'd only ever seen in vids, getting my degree and coming home to be a lecturer at University Miranda, but then reality hit me. "I'm afraid that's quite impossible, Teacher Lomas. The cost of it... My parents' farm has fine land, the cash crops give a good yield, but they have eleven children to provide for. They can't spend all their credits on me."

He nodded. "I understand, but that needn't stop you doing this, Amalie. The Education Subcommittee has arranged for our chosen students to be given a small grant from the Miranda

Planetary Development Fund, and there's also a cross-sector system where students can borrow the cost of doing their degree. You'd have to pay it back later through education tax, but that wouldn't be a problem when you've a guaranteed post waiting for you at University Miranda."

I shook my head. "But a university in another sector would never accept a student with just a Miranda Farming Studies Certificate."

He seemed to be trying not to laugh. "Oddly enough, the Education Subcommittee has thought about that issue too. All universities have a small number of places available to students under the special access scheme. This scheme was designed to assist students who come from a background that limited their educational opportunities. As a girl from a frontier world, you'd qualify for the special access scheme anyway, but with our Planetary Development Board supporting your application and stating you're a potential lecturer for one of the first universities in Epsilon sector..."

He smiled. "You don't need qualifications, Amalie. You just need to prove you have the ability to do this, and I'm already confident about that. I knew you were a very bright girl, flying through your Farming Studies Certificate incredibly quickly, so I got you reading a lot of different texts. You responded best to the history texts, so we're thinking of you as a history lecturer, though literature would also be possible if you preferred that."

"History? But why would University Miranda want a history lecturer?"

Lomas did laugh this time. "If University Miranda is going to be respected, and make our world a leading force in Epsilon sector, it has to be a proper university that teaches everything. Yes, the Agriculture Department, Medical Department, and Teacher Training Department will be the biggest to start with, but we will have many others, including a small History Department."

He stood up. "I knew this whole idea would come as a huge shock to you, Amalie, but please take a while to consider it. I'll send some more detailed information to your lookup. If you think of any questions or issues that aren't answered in that information, please message me about them."

I watched Lomas go back into the dome, and then buried my face in my hands. I'd never travelled further than Memorial. The idea of spending years on another world in a distant sector...

I was distracted by the odd, warm feeling of my right foot. I peered down at it, and saw a small, furry, Mirandan panda mouse was sitting on my foot, trying to find a way to get inside my shoe. I waved my foot in the air, the panda mouse fell off, and landed on the ground with a plaintive mooping sound of complaint. The minute I put my foot back down, the panda mouse went for the shoe again.

I groaned, picked up the panda mouse, took it over to the nearest bushes, and dumped it there. Their fascination with shoes made panda mice a perishing nuisance. My eldest brother was always threatening to stamp on the next one he found sleeping inside one of his shoes, but of course he never did. Nobody ever had the heart to hurt a panda mouse. People said that their long, black and white fur, and huge soulful eyes, meant they were nearly as appealing as a human baby. Personally, I thought that panda mice were much cuter than human babies, and had the big advantage that they didn't need their nappies changing.

I'd just gone back to the bench again, when my lookup chimed. That must be Lomas sending me the information. I tapped the screen, was startled to discover I'd actually answered an incoming call, and even more startled to recognize the male face that appeared on the display. It was a little green, because my aging lookup's colour was a bit erratic, but this was definitely Rodrish Jain, painter of pink hummingbirds.

"Amalie!" He beamed at me. "It's ready and it's wonderful. No, it's more than wonderful, it's totally zan!"

"What's ready?"

"My house! Well, not entirely ready, but the roof is on, and there are interior walls, so you can come and see it tomorrow."

Come and see it tomorrow? I had the feeling I was missing some basic facts here. I took a closer look at Rodrish's green face. "Are you drunk again?"

"Only a little," he said. "A couple of glasses of Pedra's home brewed whiskey."

"A couple of glasses of Pedra's whiskey would knock out an Asgard bison."

"I know. I was just nervous about... Chaos, I'm not doing this very well, am I?"

I grinned. "I'm not even sure what you're trying to do, so no you aren't."

"I thought I'd messed everything up falling off the roof like that. It had to be the worst offer of marriage ever, so I daren't even message you afterwards, but given you've done what I asked and waited for me to get my house built..."

Offer of marriage? I tried to remember exactly what had happened on the day of the pink hummingbird. I certainly hadn't noticed Rodrish offering me marriage. He had been shouting something before he fell off the top of the dome, but it hadn't made any sense until the final "Oh nuke!" when his foot slipped.

"Rodrish Jain, are you offering marriage to me?" I asked.

"Yes."

I wasn't sure how to react to this. Normally, I slapped down any drunken offer of marriage without even pausing to think about it, but this was Rodrish Jain, the son of one of the Founding Families of Miranda. I hesitated before saying anything.

"Rodrish, you're drunk. If you're serious about this, you'll have to ask me again when you're sober. If possible when we're face to face, rather than just calling me."

He gave a despairing shake of his head. "But I can't do this sober. I needed a couple of drinks before I had the nerve to say it in a call, and saying it in person is even worse. That's why I got so drunk on my last day at school. I kept thinking another drink would help."

I frowned. Actually, that did explain a lot. Despite being a son of one of the Founding Families, Rodrish Jain was a quiet, shy boy, who didn't drink much. One of the reasons everyone remembered the pink hummingbird episode was that it was so out of character.

"I accept you find these things difficult," I said, "but you wouldn't have to actually say it again. If you call me tomorrow, I'll take it as meaning you were serious about the offer of marriage."

"All right," said Rodrish.

"Goodbye then."

There was a very long pause. Eventually, I tried again. "Goodbye, Rodrish."

"Oh. Right." He ended the call.

I frowned down at my blank lookup screen. If Rodrish Jain was serious, and I was certain he was serious despite the two glasses of Pedra's whiskey, then my future was decided. Rodrish was a respectable, dependable boy, at least he was when he was sober, and given his parents' status...

I was going to marry Rodrish Jain. I let that thought sink in for a moment, imagining myself announcing this to my stunned family, and all the interfering neighbours who'd been nagging me about my duty to marry. I could tell them that Rodrish Jain had offered me marriage last year, but we'd been waiting for me to be 17 and for his house to be built before telling anyone.

I pictured the look of shock and embarrassment on their faces. The ones who'd made pointed remarks about me not doing my duty would feel total idiots. They'd been criticizing a girl who was already betrothed to a son of one of the Founding Families!

My lookup chimed again. I checked it and saw Lomas had sent the promised information. There was no point in me reading it now. I was staying on Miranda, and marrying Rodrish. Information about travelling to a world in another sector to study history was completely irrelevant.

I tapped my lookup, and started reading it anyway.

KAPPA SECTOR 2788 - COLONEL RIAK TORREK

Planet K21228, Kappa Sector, October 2788.

Part I

Planet K21228 was about to move from Planet First to Colony Ten stage. I stood outside our base, my back to the cluster of massive grey domes, and stared up at the sky. There was a whole list of rules for the ceremony where the Military formally handed over a new colony world to its first colonists. The first rule on the list was that it must not rain.

I couldn't see a single cloud overhead, but it was a windy day so the weather could change fast. I currently had sixteen fighters scattered across the skies of what would soon be the inhabited continent of Planet K21228. I tapped the curved shape of the Military lookup attached to the left sleeve of my uniform.

"Command Support," said the briskly efficient voice of Major Rayne Tar Cameron. "How can we assist you, Colonel?"

"Please patch me through to Major Tell Dramis," I said.

"Patching you through now, sir."

I heard the faint crackle as I was linked to the command feed. "Major Tell Dramis, can I have a status report?"

"Sir, my team report there are absolutely no signs of enemy clouds," said the cheerful voice of Drago Tell Dramis. "If we sight any hostiles, we will fire immediately!"

"This is not an appropriate subject for humour, Major!" I snapped. "Thousands of my officers have worked for years to prepare this planet for colonization. Seven of those officers died. If we get so much as one drop of rain during the hand-over ceremony, then all that effort and sacrifice will be wasted, because every colonist setting foot on this world will be scared of their own shadow."

"Colonel Torrek, sir, I'm fully aware of the importance of this," said Drago.

I ignored him. "Everyone remembers what happened to the last colony world where it rained during the handover ceremony. Every horror vid set in the nightmare of the Thetis chaos year features the sudden torrential rainstorm in the middle of the handover ceremony on Thetis. I don't want this to be the first handover ceremony in over a quarter of a millennium to..."

I broke off. There was an awkward silence, and then I sighed. "Sorry, Drago. I shouldn't have ranted at you like that but I'm a bit tense this morning. Handover ceremonies are always big moments, but this one... My last handover ceremony. My last command. My last day before retirement. Well, as I said, I'm a bit tense."

"Perfectly understandable," said Drago, "but there's no need to worry. There isn't a single cloud over this continent. My team are monitoring two cloud formations offshore, but they're both moving away from us. If the wind changes direction, then we're ready to seed them out of existence."

"Thanks, Drago."

I tapped my lookup to end the call, went inside the nearest dome, and along the corridor to my quarters. The rooms were bare and unwelcoming now that most of my per-sonal possessions had been packed away in my set of hover luggage. The only decorations left on the walls were my set of three holo portraits.

I went to stand in front of the portraits and studied them for a few minutes. I was at the end of my Military career, so it had seemed fitting to set the portraits to show images from the very start. The one on the left showed me at my Military Academy graduation almost exactly sixty years ago. Chaos, I looked impossibly young and naive, not to mention hideously uncomfortable in my dress uniform.

Both the other portraits showed images from that Military Academy graduation as well. In the centre was a laughing girl, her waist-long hair hanging loose in open defiance of the advised hair styles when wearing dress uniform. By the time we'd reached graduation, the instructors had given up arguing with her about the hair. They were just counting the seconds until she'd leave the Military Academy, and their nerves could start recovering from the strain of having her there.

Over on the right, the third portrait showed an immaculate young officer. Perfectly at ease in his dress uniform, with a correctly serious expression on his face, and proudly holding the Military Academy Shield of Honour for the cadet with the highest overall score. He was less than two months older than me, but he'd always managed to look at least three years my senior and about a decade more sophisticated. That was only one of the reasons I'd spent most of my time at the Academy wanting to murder him.

"Well," I said. "This is it. Wish me luck!"

I heard the voices in my head calling back to me. The female one was always eager and emotional. "Luck to you, Riak Torrek!" The male one had a bored, superior tone. "You can do this, farm boy!"

I took a deep breath, and called General Kpossi at Colony Ten Command. She was waiting for the call, so her image appeared on my lookup within seconds.

"Sir," I said, "Planet K21228 is now moving to first stage colonization."

"You have clear skies, Colonel?" asked General Kpossi.

"Sir, we have totally clear skies."

"Then I shall send your colonists the one hour countdown alert."

General Kpossi's image froze while she sent the standard, pre-prepared message. A group of a thousand colonists were waiting at one of the Military bases in Kappa sector. They hadn't known it, but they'd been assigned to K21228 for the last two months. Their last stage training had been specially tailored for conditions on K21228. The day and night cycle of their accommodation domes had been set to match the time zone of the prospective inhabited continent of K21228. Three days ago, they'd been moved to standby status, and since then we'd just been waiting for a sunny day to welcome them to their new home.

Colonists were never told what planet they were going to until they got the one hour alert, in case there were last minute problems with their world and they had to be reassigned. Now a thousand people were reading General Kpossi's message, and knew their new home was going to be planet K21228. Their bags were already packed. Their crates of equipment and stores, their vast stacks of flexiplas dome parts, their seed for crops, were already loaded on transport sleds. The colonists only had to get their livestock organized and they'd be ready to move out.

I had a pre-prepared message ready too. The handover ceremony was when we gave a new world to humanity. That ceremony wasn't just for the incoming civilian colonists. It was also for the Military who'd risked their lives to make that world safe.

I tapped my lookup, sending my message out to all the officers still here under my command, as well as those who'd completed their part in opening this world years ago and moved on. Many of those people had already returned to join the handover ceremony, while others were stationed in star systems close enough that they could portal here as soon as they got my message. Others were on assignments on worlds in strict quarantine, so they couldn't attend the handover ceremony, but they would be watching the vid coverage on live link.

General Kpossi's image came to life again. "Your colonists confirm they should be ready to move out on schedule. They've got one especially recalcitrant cow, but we can always ship that out to them later." She smiled. "You haven't reconsidered your position on retirement, Colonel?"

I fought the urge to groan. Last year, I'd formally registered my decision to retire at the end of this assignment. Ever since then, people had been trying to change my mind.

"No, sir," I said. "I'm 80 years old. From now on, I'll need increasingly frequent and lengthy rejuvenation treatments to keep me in good health. It's time for me to retire from active duty."

"You aren't *quite* 80 years old yet, Colonel."

"A few months make little difference, sir. The position of a Planet First commanding officer is both physically and mentally demanding. I'm no longer capable of meeting those demands. It's time for me to step down and retire."

General Kpossi shook her head. "I disagree, Colonel. You've had a long and distinguished career, but I don't believe that career should end yet. Your leadership skills inspire confidence and trust, your patience and people management skills mean you can deal with the most difficult of officers, and you've an extraordinary ability to pick the right people for any position."

"Thank you, General," I said, "but many other officers are as good at all of those things, and have the advantage of being much younger. I've done more than I ever dreamed of in my Military career, achieved a rank and position that's higher than I ever expected, deserved, or wanted. Now it's time for me to retire."

"Riak, there's no point in belittling yourself to me. I know exactly how good you are, because I served under your command myself twelve years ago. When I was struggling to cope with bereavement, you helped me to pick up the pieces of my life and career. You're the reason I'm a General now."

"I'm perfectly confident that you would have reached your current rank without my assistance," I said.

"I disagree. If you feel another Planet First assignment is too much, then have you considered something entirely different, Colonel? A post at the Military Academy perhaps?"

I was shocked, wondering how General Kpossi knew I was thinking about my days at the Military Academy, then realized the obvious. The holo portraits on the wall were in full view of my lookup.

I glanced at the portraits, pictured myself as an instructor at the Military Academy, and cringed. My every memory of the Academy was of the three of us. Going back there alone, to a place where the ghosts of my past walked every corridor, would...

"No, sir. A post at the Military Academy would be totally impossible."

General Kpossi sighed. "Well, if you think of any other type of post that might tempt you, please let me know."

"Thank you, sir. I'm afraid I really must go now. I have a handover ceremony to organize."

I was lying, my deputy was organizing the handover ceremony for me, but General Kpossi didn't know that. "Of course, Colonel."

I ended the call, went into my bedroom, changed into my dress uniform, and studied myself in the mirror. I felt I didn't just look 80, but as if I'd already reached my hundredth and was waiting to peacefully die of old age! The jacket collar was annoying me as usual. I tugged at it, which only made it worse.

I'd been told that my problems with dress uniform were entirely psychological, a lingering legacy of my struggle to make the adjustment from being a civilian to being a Military officer. It was true that dress uniforms bothered me far more when I was under stress, but I still felt the fancy design of the collar was really to blame. I avoided wearing my dress uniform whenever I could, but today it was mandatory.

I checked the time on my lookup. Still forty minutes before the handover ceremony was due to start, and I absolutely mustn't turn up early. My deputy would be frantically organizing everything, and having me watching wouldn't just distract her but make her think I didn't trust her to get this right.

I sighed, headed back out into the living room, and shook my head at the male portrait on the wall. "Don't give me that smug look. I know I'm not a walking Military Recruitment poster like you, but at least I never..."

There was a loud thump from behind me. I whirled round and discovered my apartment door was lying on the floor. A boy in a Military Cadet's uniform was standing next to it, an appalled expression on his face.

"Dreadfully sorry, sir. I was ordered to remove all the doors on this corridor. I'd no idea you were in here." He tapped the lookup on his sleeve in a blind panic, obviously double-checking his instructions. "Maybe I got the wrong..."

I peered at his lookup screen. "That says corridor D1, and this is definitely corridor D1. Please calm down, Cadet. This isn't your fault."

I tapped my own lookup, and Major Rayne Tar Cameron's face appeared. It was always Rayne who answered my calls. The woman was incredibly efficient, but she couldn't possibly answer every Command Support call herself, so my guess was she had a routing algorithm set up to send what she considered important calls directly to her.

"Command Support. How can we assist you, Colonel?"

"Rayne, can you send a message to whoever is in charge of

dismantling this base and has flagged dome D for removal? Tell them that Colonel Torrek sends his compliments, and points out that his quarters are in dome D. He will still be using those quarters until noon tomorrow, and would prefer the rooms to have the standard number of doors, walls and ceilings until then."

She blinked. "Surely they haven't actually...?"

"Just my front door, and don't worry." I glanced across at where the cadet was working on replacing the door. "Someone's already putting it back. Just try to stop it happening again."

"Yes, sir."

I ended the call and turned to the cadet. I didn't like the resigned expression on his face. I didn't know how many mistakes the boy had already made in his time at the Military Academy, but he'd reached his limit with this one. He'd given up now. As soon as he'd put my door back in place, he was going to go and tell his instructor that he was leaving the Military. I knew the signs perfectly, because I'd been through exactly the same thing myself. Even after six decades, I could still remember the feeling that I was drowning in a wave of despair and failure.

"This wasn't your fault, Cadet," I repeated. "I assume the Military Academy has sent your class here on a field assignment. We've had a lot of classes visiting in the last few months. It's good experience for cadets to visit a Planet First base, but naturally they can only come to worlds that are out of full quarantine and nearing handover stage."

Telling the boy it wasn't his fault wasn't helping. Right now, he probably felt he was personally responsible for every mistake the Military had ever made, including giving way to political pressure to clear Thetis for colonization before all the Planet First checks were properly complete.

I tried a different approach. "If your class has been dragged into helping dismantle the base, then I hope your instructor is going to let you watch the handover ceremony."

"Yes, sir. We've been told we can watch it from the hillside overlooking the..." The cadet turned his head to answer me, and dropped the door again. He groaned and stooped to pick it up.

I felt like groaning too. The boy should be wild with enthusiasm at the prospect of standing on a new planet, watching the ritual moment when it became one of the worlds of humanity. This was the dream of every cadet, but this boy had given up on his dreams and was just depressed.

"Let me hold the door steady for you," I said. "Taking doors off is always easier than putting them on again. You're a sector recruit, aren't you?"

The cadet's look of anguish deepened. "Yes, sir."

I held the door in place while he tried putting in the locking pins. He was having trouble because his hands were shaking.

"What's your name?" I asked.

"Cadet Helden Keusink, sir."

"I was a sector recruit myself," I said. "A clueless farm boy from Tethys in Gamma sector. My head was stuffed full of romantic fantasies of a Military career working for Planet First. My heart was filled with a burning hatred for carrots."

"You were a sector recruit, sir?" The cadet gave me a startled look. "I'm from Gamma sector too. Asgard, in fact."

"Then you have the great advantage that people have heard of your world, Helden. Whenever I said I was from Tethys, everyone gave me a blank look. Even the other sector recruits from Gamma sector hadn't heard of it. The only notable thing about Tethys is that carrots grow incredibly well there."

I smiled. "I'd never gone off world before I signed up for the Military. I was wildly excited to leave the carrot fields and travel all the way to Alpha sector. It took me a long time to get there. I knew so little about interstellar portal travel that I thought you had to go from Gamma sector to Alpha sector via

Beta sector, but I finally made it to Alpha Sector Interchange 1. That was when I called Military Support for help. My instructions just said to go to Academy in Alpha sector, they didn't tell me what planet the Academy was on."

Helden made an odd choking noise.

"Oh, please feel free to laugh," I said. "I don't know how the Military Captain who answered my call managed to keep a straight face, but he did. He very patiently explained to me that Academy wasn't *on* a planet, Academy *was* a planet. He told me the Military Academy, the Military Headquarters, and a lot of other Military facilities were all on the planet called Academy. Then he said I was clearly having a few problems making the journey, and offered to send someone to come and get me."

Helden made the choking noise again.

I laughed. "I hastily declined. Fortunately I had a few hours to wait before the next scheduled interstellar block portal to Academy, which gave me the chance to recover from my embarrassment. Once I got to Academy, I actually managed to enter the local portal code I'd been given and get to the basic training area without getting lost again. I was put in a class with thirty-two other sector recruits. I was bottom of the class at absolutely everything, but it's impossible to fail basic training so I carried on to be formally enrolled as a Military Academy cadet."

I paused. "Things got even worse at that point. All the sector recruits were split up and put in classes with the huge majority of cadets who came from Military families. They seemed to know everything already, and the second I opened my mouth they all knew I was a sector recruit. I hated that. Don't you?"

"Oh yes, sir!" said Helden. "I feel like I've got a label on my forehead."

"It's mostly the sector accent that gives you away. The cadets from Military families speak Language without any accent at all. You will too after a couple of years in the Military."

I shrugged. "Once I was at the Military Academy itself, I was even more disastrously bad at everything than during basic training. At the end of the first week, I decided to tell my class instructor I was quitting the Military. I'd done my best, and I'd failed. I was going to give up, go back home, and grow carrots after all."

Helden frowned. "But you didn't?"

I shook my head. "Two of my classmates caught me as I was about to knock on our instructor's door. They guessed what was going on, dragged me back to my quarters, and barricaded me in."

I pointed at the holo portraits on the wall. "That's the three of us. I'm the confused looking one on the left of course, not the perfect Military officer on the right."

The cadet stared at the portraits, and gave me a bemused look as if he couldn't believe I'd ever been that young.

"They said the whole class would get in trouble if I quit," I said, "and refused to let me out of my room until I promised to give it another month. After that, they made it their mission in life to turn a farm boy into a Military officer."

"That's the other thing, sir," said the cadet. "Since less than 10 per cent of cadets are sector recruits, the Military have strict rules about making us feel welcome. I know my instructor and my classmates must think I'm an idiot, but they have to hide it and be nice to me or they'll be put on report."

He waved a hand at the door. "Just look at this job, sir. My classmates are dismantling a dome full of science labs, and packing away delicate equipment. I nearly broke something hideously expensive by trying to force it into the wrong storage box. Anyone else would have had the instructor yelling at them, while the rest of the class stood around laughing, but I just got sent over here to take off doors. The instructor thought even I couldn't get that wrong, but..."

"What you have to remember is that cadets from Military families have got a huge head start on you," I said. "You had a few months of basic training before you started at the Military Academy. They've had eighteen years of living on Military bases and going to Military schools. All that time, they've been absorbing knowledge."

I wondered if this was a good moment to mention that Helden shouldn't be calling me "sir" any longer. I'd called him by his first name, which showed I'd changed this from a formal to an informal conversation, a perfect example of something a cadet from a Military family would know but Helden didn't.

I decided I'd better not risk it. "Your instructor knows that," I continued, "and your classmates know it too. That's why they don't make fun of you. It's not because they're scared of being put on report. It's because you don't gloat at beating someone in a race when you know they've had to run twice as far as you."

Helden finished attaching the door, stepped back and looked at it disconsolately. "Perhaps you're right, sir, but it doesn't make much difference now anyway. I have to forget all about graduating the Military Academy and taking the Military Oath of Service, because I'll never live this down. I've taken the door off a Colonel's quarters, while the Colonel was inside them!"

"You were just following orders," I said. "Tell your class-mates about it, and watch their faces. You'll see a look of horror, because they know it could have happened to them as easily as you."

I paused. "Anyway, everyone has embarrassing incidents to live down. Take me for example. I burned down a dome once."

Helden looked shocked. "At the Military Academy, sir?"

"No, this was later," I said. "I was a Captain on a Planet First assignment, and I'd had rather an... intense day. The

144

three of us had been out in an armour-plated Field Command sled, collecting samples for the scientists, when we ran into a big herd of some local wildlife. Rather like Asgard bison, but with bigger teeth and extremely bad tempers. We were in a small valley, with the herd blocking the only way out. The real problems began when the herd noticed our sled, and started playing games with it. They couldn't get through the armour plating, but they could roll the sled over and push it around."

Helden's eyes got even wider.

I shrugged. "We screamed for help, the fighter team came to the rescue, and there was a period of utter chaos while they chased off the herd. Somewhere in the middle of that, I proposed marriage to two Betans."

Helden blinked.

"Or possibly they proposed marriage to me," I said. "They'd been trying to persuade me into a triad relationship for ages, but I'd been refusing. I was from a very conventional Gamman background, and I wanted to be twoing with the girl, not sharing her with a third party, especially a third party that kept calling me farm boy!"

I waved a dismissive hand. "Well, maybe I proposed to them, or maybe they proposed to me. As I said, it was utter chaos at the time, so none of us were ever quite sure of the details. All that mattered was that I'd reached the point where I gave in and accepted there'd be three of us rather than two."

I grinned at the portraits on the wall. This was our long running private joke. At every possible chance, I'd complain about being forced into Threeing rather than Twoing. Then he'd say...

The male voice in my head said the words. "You know you love me really, farm boy!"

"I don't know why I was fool enough to get involved with either of you, when I could have married the amazing Pascal instead!" The female voice in my head completed our comedy routine.

Pascal had undoubtedly been the brightest cadet in our class, brilliant academically, but useless at anything remotely practical. He'd wisely opted to train as a Military Science Specialist rather than becoming combat Military. I'd lost track of his career after he was assigned to a joint civilian and Military research project. I wondered what had become of him later on, whether he was still...

I saw Helden was giving me an odd look, so I hurried on with my story. "Once we were safely back at base, the Medical team patched us up, and then the three of us celebrated by getting totally powered. Everything was fine until I had the bright idea of setting off some distress flares."

I paused. "Unfortunately, I set off the distress flares inside one of our domes. Never do that, Helden. It's a really bad idea. By the time our fire crews put the blaze out, there wasn't an awful lot of the dome left. Luckily it was one of the smallest domes, but our commanding officer was still rather upset about it. Now I'm a commanding officer myself, I can quite see his point. Anyway, what I'm telling you is that everyone has their embarrassing moments to live down, and taking off the wrong door is a rather minor issue compared with burning down a dome."

"I suppose that's true, sir," said Helden.

"You've obviously got as far as realizing the Military work desperately hard to encourage sector recruits, but I don't think you understand the reason."

Helden pulled a face. "I thought it was pity."

I shook my head. "It's because you can contribute something to the Military that your classmates can't. What's the most important job of the Military, Helden?"

"Planet First, sir. Making new worlds safe for humanity."

"That's what every civilian thinks, and it's what the original Military Charter said. That was written at the start of the twenty-fourth century, when the only two inhabited worlds were Earth and Adonis. Once there were hundreds of inhabited worlds, the Military became the cross-sector Military, and the Military Charter was completely re-written with new priorities."

I smiled. "The new Military Charter states the prime objective of the Military is to maintain the peace between the worlds of humanity. It specifies that the cross-sector Military must remain politically neutral, recruit from all worlds without prejudice, and do everything possible to promote the bonds of understanding between different worlds and cultures."

I paused. "There's a lot about Planet First as well, but that's the second priority. Offering new worlds to humanity is far less important than stopping wars between those we already have. That makes sense, doesn't it?"

Helden thought that over. "Yes, sir."

"So the primary objective of the Military is to be a unifying force between over a thousand worlds, and particularly between the distinctive cultures of the sectors of humanity. The problem is that we have a largely hereditary Military, with its own culture and traditions. Pure practicalities, like the need to keep new worlds under strict quarantine until they're proved to be safe, mean that many Military officers will have little contact with civilians. The Military can't promote bonds of understanding between civilian cultures unless its officers understand those cultures themselves."

I pointed at Helden. "That's why the Military needs people like you. Sector recruits are the glue that holds everything together, because they renew the links between the Military and the sectors. You aren't just at the Military Academy to learn, Helden, but to teach. That's why the sector recruits are put in the same classes as cadets with Military background. You're teaching your fellow cadets and your instructors too, about civilian life and about the latest cultural attitudes in Gamma sector."

"Oh." Helden considered that.

"You see your civilian background as a problem," I said, "but actually it makes you immensely valuable. So please give yourself a while longer before you abandon the Military life. You never know, you might end up being a Colonel yourself one day. On the whole, I feel I've had a better life in the Military than I'd have had growing carrots."

I thought I'd said enough, and if the boy did still try and quit the Military he'd get at least three more people giving him the same lecture. I nodded at him, headed off down the corridor to the nearest base internal portal, selected my destination, and stepped through. I was still going to be a little early for the handover ceremony, but I was getting nervous. If my deputy was having any problems, I should be there to help her.

Part II

I arrived in the centre of a large area of grassland. Ahead of me, a vast mob of Military officers in dress uniform were milling around, grabbing their chance to exchange news with old friends who they hadn't seen in months or even years. Over to my left, my deputy, Commander Nia Stone, was deep in conversation with her husband, my Threat team leader, Commander Mason Leveque.

"Well, tell her she can't," said Commander Stone. "I can't let everyone pick and choose where they stand during the ceremony. I've put her in group 3 Alpha, and she's staying in group 3 Alpha!"

"The problem is you've got her ex-wife in group 3 Alpha too," said Commander Leveque.

"Ex-wife?" Commander Stone shook her head. "When did that happen? They seemed perfectly happy when they left here three months ago, and I didn't get a notification they should be kept apart."

"Apparently the divorce is due to be finalized today, so there are bound to be some intense emotions on both sides," said Commander Leveque. "I strongly advise we keep them apart, or I estimate there's a 3 per cent risk that this becomes the first handover ceremony in history where a murder is committed."

"I suppose we could swap..."

Commander Stone noticed me at this point, broke off her sentence, and saluted. Judging from her expression, I was about as welcome as a Cassandrian skunk.

I gave her a placating smile. "I see you have everything under control, Commander Stone. I'll leave you to it."

I headed over to lurk by a flag of humanity, and took a furtive look round. There was no podium or chairs, but that was traditional for a handover ceremony. Large amounts of furniture tended to spoil the untouched planet effect.

The flags were in the correct position. There were strategically placed officers controlling the small hovering spheres of vid bees. The areas of grass where the Military formations should stand had been carefully mown to mark out the group positions. I knew we hadn't managed the ultimate sin of forgetting the crystal presentation globe, because Commander Leveque was holding it.

Commander Stone decided it was time to get the mob in order. "Places everyone!" Her highly magnified voice boomed out across the grassland, and the mob of Military started sorting themselves out into squares.

Oh chaos, I hadn't remembered to wear a microphone! I whirled round in panic, wondering whether to run for the nearest portal or try to find someone else with a microphone I could borrow, and nearly collided with a Military Support Captain. He dodged sideways, pinned a microphone to my collar, and then hurried off.

I relaxed. Commander Stone really did have everything under control, even her idiot commanding officer.

"If you aren't in your designated place, get there now!" shouted Commander Stone. "We're opening the cross-sector live link of the ceremony in five minutes, and several major newzie channels will be showing live scenes."

I guiltily hurried over to stand in the neatly mown circle of grass that marked the focal point of the ceremony. A huge flag of humanity hovered in midair above me. Commander Leveque came to stand to my left, and Commander Stone gave a last harassed look around.

"Group B1, neaten your rows up, you look like a bunch of civilian school children! The vid coverage of this ceremony will be replayed every year on this world, so everything has to be perfect." She paused and checked her lookup. "Stop gossiping now, everyone. Live link is opening in three minutes. Anthem will start playing ten seconds later. Colony Ten Command confirm incoming colonists one minute after that. Attention!"

I sneaked a look over my shoulder. The square formations of Military had gone to attention. Commander Stone moved to stand at my right hand side. I hastily straightened to attention myself.

There was a long pause and then the anthem started playing. I saw something moving overhead, had a ghastly moment when I thought it was a cloud, then saw it was just a flock of pale-pink, gossamer skimmers. Since we'd eliminated the big flying lizards that hunted them, there were much larger flocks of the delicate, seed-eating, gossamer skimmers now. That was going to be a potential problem for farmers trying to grow certain crops, but having gossamer skimmers eating the farmers' crops was a lot better than having giant lizards eating the farmers.

The three freight portals ahead of us flashed to life in unison, and people started flooding through. Some arrived as couples holding hands, while others came through singly. All of them were under 30 years old, except for the older couple at the front. Those two would have been Colony Ten founding colonists on one world already. They'd spent ten years working out how to deal with that world's minor problems, and proving it was safe to be opened for full colonization. Now they were here to repeat that experience, this time as leaders of this Colony Ten group.

It took a while for all the colonists to come through the portals. It wasn't just people arriving; there were a symbolic selection of Earth animals too. I spotted horses, chickens, pigs, goats, and a few cows arriving. I wondered if the cow that kept bucking its head, trying to shake off its halter, was the recalcitrant one that General Kpossi had mentioned.

The music had changed from anthem to hymn now. When the last few colonists had arrived through the portals, the hymn hit the high note and ended. Military and civilians all saluted the flag of humanity.

I gave the traditional speech of welcome after that, the one that half of humanity could probably recite from memory, and I saw the colonists tense as I reached the key point. Not a single planet had reached Colony Ten stage without at least one member of the Military dying. The colonists were waiting to hear the human cost of giving them their world. How many names were they going to hear? The lists were usually either very short or dreadfully long, because when things started going wrong on a Planet First mission they could rapidly spiral out of control.

In most of those cases, the world was abandoned, but sometimes the scientists came up with an effective solution and it was eventually colonized. Sobek in Epsilon sector was the most famous recent example. Reciting the names at that handover ceremony had taken hours.

I started reciting names, with the standard ten second pause between each, and saw the colonists react with relief when the seventh name was followed by the traditional words. "They died to offer new worlds to humanity."

Then there was the two minutes' silence. I knew exactly what the colonists were thinking during that silence. Every new world had its memorial to the Military who made it safe for colonization. That listed the names of all the Military who'd worked on that world, but the centre point of the memorial was always the names of those who'd died. This world wouldn't be another Sobek. This world would have a mercifully short list of names.

After the silence, Commander Leveque passed me the crystal globe. I lifted it up and held it still for a full minute, so the hovering vid bees could capture the lines carved into its surface. Those lines showed the shapes of the continents of K21228, with the continent we stood on delicately inlaid in gold.

Finally, I lowered the globe, the two leaders of the colonists stepped forward, and I literally handed them their new world.

"What are you naming this world?" I asked.

The man accepted the globe, and the woman smiled. "This world is called Maia," she said.

I nodded. "May the sun shine brightly on Maia."

On cue to the second, a team of sixteen fighters swooped in over the hills, trailing sparkling bands of gold dust across the sky.

The portals flared to life again now. The Military squares started moving in turn, marching in formation to the portals, then dividing into three columns to step through. Finally Commander Stone, Commander Leveque, and I were the only Military left. We saluted, marched to the central portal and stepped through.

The vid bees would still be in position, their images showing the colonists and their animals now. In a few minutes, the transport sleds would arrive through the portals, and the colonists would start building the domes they'd need for shelter tonight. The Military had all gone now. The colonists had been left on their new world to cope alone for the next ten years.

Except, of course, that was just a romantic myth. The Colony Ten years were a carefully planned process, involving gradual introduction of Earth livestock and crops into an alien world with its own ecology. A group of Military scientists and a full Medical team had already moved into their Colony Ten Support dome, and would be helping the colonists through any problems they faced.

And the rest of the Military hadn't gone at all. We'd portalled back to our base, arriving outside the huge central dome. Nobody would leave until tomorrow, because there was still one very important thing to happen. The handover party!

Most people were already heading into the domes to get ready for that party, but I stood still for a moment, letting the tension ease away. I heard a sigh from next to me. Someone else was suffering the aftermath of tension too. I turned to smile at Commander Stone. "The ceremony went perfectly, Commander. Well done."

"Thank you, sir."

I glanced from her to Commander Leveque. "You two go and get ready for the party now, while I call the terrifying General Hiraga."

The two of them went into the dome, and I tapped my lookup. The face of a young Captain appeared on the screen. "Planet First Central Command Support," he said.

"Colonel Torrek calling General Hiraga," I said.

There was a brief pause before the image changed to show General Hiraga.

"Sir, K21228 has left Planet First and moved to Colony Ten jurisdiction," I said. "Requesting permission to officially stand down our Planet First teams."

She nodded. "Permission granted, Colonel. Excellent handover ceremony. A little minor disruption from a cow at one point, but I imagine the cow hadn't had the benefit of Military training."

I dutifully smiled. "No, sir." I paused for a second before pointedly adding. "The handover ceremony was completely organized by Commander Stone."

I waited to see if General Hiraga would say anything, but she didn't. "I hope that addresses your concerns about Commander Stone's administrational skills, sir," I added.

She kept me in suspense for another thirty seconds before nodding. "I believe it does. I shall add Commander Stone's name to the list of approved candidates for promotion to full Colonel."

My smile was genuine this time. "Thank you, sir."

The step from Commander to Colonel was notorious for being the hardest promotion to achieve in the Military. You could earn that promotion in one of three ways. Some were forced into the role of acting commanding officer by a disaster on a Planet First mission, and proved their brilliance by getting a nightmare situation under control. I'd had the easy route, being carried along in the wake of someone that brilliant. Nia Stone had done it by pure hard work.

"That information must remain strictly confidential for now though, Colonel," said General Hiraga. "Stone will have to wait for a suitable opening for a Planet First command before she gets her promotion. And by suitable, I mean that it has to be a command on a planet that's already in a reasonably stable state. Stone's not had any experience as an acting commanding officer in a crisis situation, and I'm not giving the Planet First command of a raw new world to someone totally green."

She paused. "Once we've found Stone a post, we'll need to arrange a position for her husband too, but Leveque could take the role of either Threat team leader or deputy commanding officer. It should be possible to free up one of those positions with standard personnel transfers."

I nodded. I had no concerns about that side of things at all. Since few civilians considered crossing the huge divide between civilian and Military life, it was absolutely vital for the Military to do everything it could to help its officers to maintain their relationships and raise the children who would mostly join the Military themselves. Once Stone had her command, I knew Leveque would join her there within weeks, even if a temporary position had to be created for him.

"It may be some time before there's an appropriate opening," said General Hiraga. "You could help me out with that. Delay retiring for a while, and take another Planet First command. As soon as I agree your planet is stable, you can hand your command to Stone."

I was annoyed by the blatant attempt at emotional blackmail, but I mustn't lose my temper with General Hiraga. It wouldn't harm me, I was retiring within hours, but it might damage Nia's chances.

"Sir, getting a new planet stable would take at least two to three years, perhaps far longer. I'd hope a suitable post will arise for Commander Stone well before that, so I'd rather continue with my retirement as planned."

General Hiraga sighed. "If you insist, Colonel. I suppose your handover party will be starting now. Is Commander Stone organizing that too?"

"No, sir." I enjoyed watching Hiraga's face as I told her the bad news. "Major Drago Tell Dramis volunteered to organize the party."

General Hiraga shuddered. "I just hope there's a planet left at the end of it."

I ended the call, and headed to my quarters. To my relief, I discovered they were still intact, though the front door was sagging a bit on its hinges. I thankfully changed back into my ordinary uniform, and went to stand in front of the three holo portraits.

"The handover ceremony went beautifully." I pulled a face at the exemplary Military officer in the right hand portrait, and imitated his lazy voice. "Farm boy did well. I..."

My lookup chimed. I checked the screen, saw it was Drago Tell Dramis, and accepted the call.

"We're nearly ready, sir," he said.

"I'm on my way."

I headed across to the central dome, and found it had been transformed. All the partitions for rooms and corridors had been removed to leave one massive, echoing space. It should have been dark and gloomy, but glowing, colourful abstract images were projected on the curving, grey flexiplas interior of the dome, and the floor was covered by speckles of gold. Overhead, tiny gold suns drifted around, casting random pools of light beneath them.

It all looked both spectacular and horribly familiar. Naturally it would look familiar. Every handover party stole ideas from ones that came before it, I'd gone to a lot of handover parties in six decades, and even helped organize a few. My memories of the first ones were pure joyful exuberance, only tempered by the awareness that I mustn't get powered enough to set off any distress flares. At least, not inside a dome!

Later, the three of us had been old enough and senior enough to at least try to behave ourselves, and then...

In the last twenty years, I'd been to a couple of handover parties, but I hadn't stayed long at any of them. I'd give this one an hour or two before I went to hide in my quarters.

I shook away the memories, and looked around for Drago. The dome was already filling up with people, some wearing their Military uniforms and others in distinctive clothes specific to various sectors or worlds. Most of the people wearing those clothes wouldn't have been born on those worlds themselves, but their ancestors had. One of the ways the Military kept its links to the sectors, was to encourage its officers to maintain their diverse cultural heritage. A handover party was one of the classic situations where that diversity showed.

Drago came over to meet me, looking resplendent in a Betan toga. "What do you think of the decor, sir?"

"Excellent job." I pointed at the floor. "Are the gold specks the same dust you used in the flypast at the handover ceremony?"

He grinned. "Yes. Commander Leveque advised us how to mix it with glue and spray it onto the floor."

I smiled. "I'm delighted to hear my Threat team leader has been entering into the party spirit."

"Permission to give the five minute warning, sir?"

"Permission granted, Major."

Drago tapped at his lookup. I clenched my hands and braced myself. I told myself I was ready for the base sirens to go off, just the way they did at the start of every handover party. I told myself they wouldn't be screaming alarm signals, but sounding the lighthearted notes of the base stand down. I told myself it wouldn't affect me this time, but of course it did.

The second the first note sounded, I was nearly two decades back in time. The sirens were blaring out the evacuation sequence, and I was being dragged along the floor of a corridor. Both of my legs had been smashed to pieces despite the protection of my impact suit, and the man dragging me had lost part of one arm. I was screaming at him to leave me, but he somehow got me to the portal and thrust me through.

I'd arrived in an emergency evacuation centre, been grabbed by a triage doctor, and then waved on to an officious medical team. It was two years before I forgave them for saving my life. It was three years before I was anything remotely like a functional human being. It was four years before I wore a Military uniform again.

I'd built a new life since then, and it worked after a fashion, but I kept a defensive wall between it and my old one. I kept in touch with a few people, some ties went too deep to break, but things could never be the same now I was alone. Parties were just one of the things I'd left behind me.

I came back to the present and found Drago staring at me with a face filled with concern. "Are you all right, sir?" he asked.

"I'm fine," I said, in what I hoped was a brisk voice. "You'd better go and get ready for the vid show."

"Yes, sir."

Drago gave me a last doubtful look, but dutifully went away. Civilians led nice, safe lives, and could expect to celebrate their hundredth before dying. Things were very different for the Military. A lot of officers lived with bereavement or mental scars, and the Military convention was to show respect by quietly accepting occasional oddities without pushing for painful explanations.

I hoped that these days the only outward sign of my past problems was my odd reaction to base sirens. I kept my conversations with dead people to the privacy of my quarters, but Commander Stone openly addressed comments to the ceilings or walls. By now, the whole base must have worked out that she was talking to someone she'd loved and lost, but only her husband, myself as her commanding officer, and our Medical team leader needed to know it was her twin sister.

The lights of the floating suns were dimming now, and an image of Maia from space was projected on a special flat section of wall. Blue and white, like all of the carefully selected colony worlds of humanity. When the image changed to the flag of humanity, everyone in the dome, in uniform or not, saluted.

My own voice started speaking, recorded from the handover ceremony, reciting seven names. There was a face displayed on the wall for each name, and then the screen changed to show an image of me holding up the crystal globe. The woman colonist's voice rang out around the dome.

"This world is called Maia."

Then the music started, and everyone relaxed. The solemnities were over, and it was time to remember the moments that had either been funny at the time, or we could laugh at now we knew they'd ended happily. The vid began by showing a member of the Science team, staring at a screen of technical information.

"This is odd," he said. "Sample 2782/94223 is virtually identical to an Earth apple."

Another scientist stepped into view, his face outraged. "That's not a sample! That's part of my lunch!"

Everyone laughed, and another vid clip started. A group of Military scientists and Commander Leveque were frowning at a small furry creature lying in the corner of a cage.

"It's not like Mabelle to just lie there like that," said one of the scientists. "She always comes to say hello and beg for an extra treat. She's making these odd squeaking noises too. Do you think she's ill?"

At this point, the small furry creature stood up, revealing what was underneath her.

"I think there's a 100 per cent probability Mabelle has had babies," said Leveque.

I heard Commander Stone's laughter join with mine, and turned to see that she and her husband had come to stand next to me.

"It's been a pleasure serving with you, sir," said Leveque. "You haven't changed your mind about retiring?"

I'd been asked that question a lot lately, but never by Leveque. My Threat team leader was a tactical expert, and had waited until now to ask me about my retirement plans, because he knew this would be my weakest moment. I'd spent a long time living and working with the people laughing at the vid clips. I was feeling emotional and it was very tempting to say that yes, I'd changed my mind. I could accept another Planet First command, keep a lot of my officers together, move on to another world, but...

I shook my head. "It's time to step down."

The next vid clip was of an outside view of the base, obviously taken by one of the external surveillance cameras. It showed one of the large freight portals we used to portal armoured sleds out to collect samples from distant locations.

Drago's recorded voice started speaking. Unfortunately, we didn't have any vid coverage from his aircraft for this. The vid bee attached to its nose had been eaten.

"I can see one of the flying lizards hovering just clear of the trees. It looks like a very small one. Well, relatively small. Maybe a third the size of an armoured car. If I shoot that one, it should fall on open ground. I'll be able to collect the body with a lift beam, and bring it back to base."

"No!" shouted the real Drago. "What unspeakable person sneaked this into the vid sequence?"

"The unspeakable person was me!" called the voice of Drago's deputy, Captain Marlise Weldon.

"Well, take it out right now, Captain. That's an order!"

"I'm afraid it's too late to make changes, sir," said Marlise, in an unconvincingly regretful voice. "The entire sequence has been viewed and approved by the Colonel."

Drago groaned. "Please, someone have mercy and shoot me. I don't..."

The end of his sentence was drowned out by his own recorded voice. "Commencing my attack run now, and..."

There was a weird, high-pitched shriek, followed by Drago's voice shouting. "Oh chaos! The lizards aren't loners after all. This one's called its friends for help."

My own voice was speaking now. "Get out of there fast, Major."

"Leaving as fast as possible, sir, but there's a whole mob chasing me, at least twenty of the largest ones. Even if I leave them well behind, there's a chance they can follow me by scent. I can't risk leading them all back to base."

I felt my recorded voice sounded impressively calm. The way I remembered this I'd been starting to panic. We'd lost an armoured car to just one of these lizards, so twenty of them... "We'll activate peripheral freight portal 3 for you, Major. Location should be appearing on your main display now. Fly through that to take a shortcut home, and you should definitely shake off your hostiles."

"Banking to head for portal now." There was a short pause before Drago spoke again. "Eighty seconds from portal. Chaos take it, those lizards are fast. They're losing ground at the moment, but I'll have to slow to a crawl to fly through the portal. I might get a fighter through at speed, but this is a combination transport so it's a really tight fit. Shut down the portal connection the second I'm through, because they'll be very close behind me."

"We'll be ready to shut down the portal, Major," I said, "and we're sending out a reception committee in case any lizards make it through with you."

The image on the wall showed impact suit clad figures running out to man the massive base laser cannons. The big freight portal was active now, lights flashing.

"Thirty seconds to portal," said Drago, "and... Oh nuke! The ones chasing me must still be calling for assistance, because there's more coming from ahead, blocking my route to the portal. Some closing from the sides too. I'll have to try and shoot my way through the ones ahead to reach the portal."

My voice wasn't saying anything now, because there was nothing helpful I could say. The vid images showed the laser cannons had swung round to aim at the portal.

"Firing now," said Drago.

There was a period where we couldn't hear anything except strange thumps and rending noises. This was the point where the vid bee got eaten. For a minute there, we'd thought Drago had been eaten as well.

Finally, Drago's voice gasped. "Coming through. Lost lateral thrusters. Got a passenger."

An aircraft flew in through the portal and slid across the ground at high speed. Well, most of an aircraft. Part of the left side had ripped off against the edge of the portal, and a giant lizard was hanging on to the right side, gouging holes with a combination of teeth and claws. The portal exploded in a shower of sparks, just as the lizard lost its grip, went tumbling sideways, and was instantly blasted to pieces by the base laser cannons.

Loud cheers rang round the dome as the vid clip ended.

"It's true what everyone says," called out Marlise Weldon. "Drago really is irresistibly handsome. At least, he's irresistibly handsome to giant flying lizards!"

"Have mercy," pleaded Drago. "Start the next vid clip."

The next vid clip duly started, but my mind was still on the lizards. We'd had to go for global extermination in the end, because the nightmare things could migrate between continents. Global extermination was always a last resort because of the potential ecological consequences, but it was that or abandon K21228.

"I still can't believe Drago got that aircraft through the portal, let alone survived uninjured," muttered Nia Stone from next to me. "I've tried it myself on a simulator twenty times. Even with the variable wings fully swept back, the aircraft barely fits through by itself, and with the lizard clinging to one side..."

"Drago had to collide with one side of the portal or the other," said Leveque. "The weight of the lizard was already spinning his aircraft to that side and he had no lateral thrusters to correct the spin. The natural instinct would be to hit the lizard into the side of the portal, try to kill it or at least make it let go, but the impact would spin the aircraft even further so he wouldn't make it through the portal."

Leveque shrugged. "Drago had to fight his instinct, and deliberately hit the other side of the portal, so losing his aircraft wing would straighten his angle of flight, and the cockpit would make it through the portal intact. If he got it right, his impact suit would protect him in the crash landing, but the margin for error was impossibly small."

My lookup chimed. I answered the call, but half the crowd was still shouting out teasing remarks aimed at Drago. I could see the head and shoulders of a Major on the screen, but I didn't recognize the man, and I couldn't hear a word he was saying.

I headed out of the nearest door, and there was sudden quiet as it closed behind me. Planet First domes were built with reinforced walls to defend against hostile wildlife, so they blocked the sound of even the loudest party.

"Sorry, Major," I said. "It was very noisy in there. What did you say?"

"General Staff Central Command Support," said the Major. "General May sends his compliments and asks if it's convenient to talk to you."

I blinked. It wasn't just that this was the third General talking to me in one day. I'd never had any contact with General May before, and why would a member of the General Staff be calling me anyway?

"It's convenient," I said.

Part III

"Transferring the call now," said the Major.

A moment later, a face appeared on my lookup screen. If anything, this General was even older than me. If he was calling to try and talk me out of retiring, then he might not accept my age as a good reason.

"Colonel Torrek," he said, "I was fascinated to read the notes you attached to the personnel record of Major Drago Tell Dramis."

I wasn't sure what I'd expected this call to be about, but it certainly wasn't that! "You mean the notes marked for the attention of his next commanding officer?"

"That's right," said General May. "I'm particularly intrigued by the part where you say that some details are difficult to explain in a report and suggest his future commanding officer calls you to discuss them."

I hesitated. "I'm not clear how you came to read the notes, sir."

"Part of my duties involves monitoring the career progression of certain officers," said General May. "Major Drago Tell Dramis has had an extremely interesting career progression. Officers usually work their way up the ranks of the Military, however Drago Tell Dramis manages to progress both up and down. If it was humanly possible, I expect he'd go sideways as well."

I gave the obligatory polite smile in response to a senior officer making a joke, but didn't say a word. I still wasn't sure what was going on here.

"You seem to have stabilized him a little," added the General, "because he's held the rank of Major for nearly two years now. I even had hopes you'd manage to promote him to

Commander, but I see from your notes that you were deliberately avoiding doing that."

He gave me an expectant look, and I felt I had to say something. "Judging from his history, I thought he'd come up with a creative way to force me to demote him again. I've been following the alternative tactic of giving him the post of a Commander, but not the rank. May I ask why you're monitoring his career, sir?"

"It started with an incident during the comet blockade on Hera," said General May. "You're familiar with the events there?"

"To a certain extent."

"The smaller incoming comet debris was easily destroyed by fighters, but the comet core itself was heading straight for the inhabited continent of Hera. Most of the population had been evacuated, but a few thousand had stubbornly refused to leave. If the comet core struck the inhabited continent then it would kill those people, and quite probably leave that area of the planet uninhabitable in future. The comet core was coming in at an angle that meant the Hera solar array couldn't be used against it, so we sent every fighter team assigned to the blockade to try to destroy it with one huge combined missile attack. The comet core exploded, but one large fragment survived the attack and was still on course for the inhabited continent."

He paused. "The fighters were out of missiles, but Lieutenant Tell Dramis's fighter collided with the comet fragment, changing its course just enough for it to pass within range of the Hera solar array, which was then able to destroy it. Lieutenant Tell Dramis claimed this collision was a complete accident."

"He's still claiming that, sir," I said.

"Do you believe him, Colonel?"

"No, sir. I don't. I've just been watching a vid of the man perform an absolutely impossible feat of flying. Every pilot in the base has tried duplicating it in a simulator, including me. It was hardly surprising I couldn't do it, I'm horribly out of practice, but all the other fighter pilots took several attempts before they could even get close to making it. I can't believe the same man ever flew straight into a rock by accident."

"You'll understand that what happened at Hera attracted the attention of higher command. Lieutenant Tell Dramis was promoted, and his personnel record flagged for special monitoring." General May frowned. "You appear to disapprove of that, Colonel Torrek. I'd like you to speak your thoughts freely."

"Exactly how freely would you like me to speak, sir?" I asked.

"Would it help if I assure you I was not involved in the decisions made after Hera, and this conversation will remain totally private between the two of us?"

I gave in. I'd been wanting to say this to someone, and given I was retiring... "Drago's promotion was badly mishandled, sir. Anyone making a unique contribution that helps resolve a critical situation, whether that's an idea that no one else could have suggested or an action that no one else could have performed, is rewarded with a promotion. Everyone understands that. The problem was that Drago wasn't promoted to Captain, but straight to Major."

"Promoting him to Captain would have been meaningless," said General May. "Lieutenant isn't a real rank. It's a label saying you've just graduated the Military Academy. Everyone who isn't completely incompetent will get promoted to Captain after the end of their six month active service acclimatization period."

"I can see that, sir, but it would still have been better to be creative about it, make an excuse to delay giving Drago his extra promotion until after he'd made the natural progression to Captain, rather than having him jump over the rank of Captain entirely. With anyone else, it probably wouldn't have mattered, but there was an extra factor in Drago's case that made it a really bad idea."

"Please explain the extra factor to me, Colonel," said General May.

I sighed. "I should explain I have personal connections to his family."

"I'm perfectly aware of that, Colonel. It's why I arranged for Major Tell Dramis to be posted to your command. I'm not clear about your exact relationship, frankly I find Betan family relationships deeply confusing, but I hoped your inside knowledge would help you deal with him."

"Oh." I'd thought Drago's team arriving on K21228 two years ago had been random chance, but... "Yes, given triad marriages are common, Betan relationships can get confusing, especially when there's divorce and re-marriage involved. They have several hundred Betan dialect terms to describe all the possible relationships."

I smiled. "Personally, I always took the easy way out, and called someone cousin rather than risk using the wrong term. The key thing to remember is that all three members of a triad marriage are both legally and culturally regarded as parents of any children, regardless of the actual genetic relationship. This means you can end up in the situation where, for example, first cousins have no genetic relationship at all. The Betan clans keep detailed family trees with full genetic data so it's clear which family members are free to marry each other."

"I see," said General May, in the voice of someone who was still totally confused.

"Anyway, the relationship between Drago and myself is one of the simpler ones. There's no genetic link between us, but he's my great-nephew by triad marriage. That gives me certain advantages in dealing with him. I'm not just his commanding officer, but a senior member of his family, and nearly 80 years old. That combination puts immense Betan cultural pressure on Drago to treat me with the deepest respect. As for inside knowledge..."

I shrugged. "I've been rather distant from the clan for the last two decades, but I'm still in contact with some of them, and hear most of the family news. As I said, there was an extra factor that made Drago's double promotion a bad idea. To be frank, the extra factor was Drago's father."

I paused to give General May a wary look.

"Please continue, Colonel," he said.

"You may be aware that General Dragon Tell Dramis is a forceful man," I said. "When he wants something he pushes hard, and he's been pushing Drago since he was 2 years old. Telling the boy he has to live up to his heroic ancestors and his father's example, and have a brilliant Military career. I'm not sure exactly what went through Drago's head when he got that double promotion, but it wouldn't surprise me if he thought his father was behind it, trying to give him a high speed start to his career."

General May gave me a startled look. "That would be impossible. Military officers are automatically excluded from promotion decisions involving partners or close relatives."

"I know that, but if Drago was feeling paranoid... Anyway, something Drago let slip last year makes me believe he decided to find out the truth about his promotion. Drago's notoriously handsome. I think he talked someone in Military Personnel into letting him look at his confidential personnel record. I can just imagine him charming them into submission. After all, what could possibly be the harm in letting Drago look at his *own* record?"

General May groaned.

"My theory is he saw a few extremely confidential notes about startling tactical ability and potential for high rank. Perhaps even a projected career path, with target ranks for him to reach at certain ages. He was fresh from the Military

Academy, and what he saw scared him to death. He's been fighting promotion ever since."

There was a short silence before General May spoke. "Your theory isn't entirely untenable."

What he meant was that I was precisely right about Drago's records. I knew it!

"The incident at Hera attracted the attention of the General Marshal and his General Staff," said General May. "We had the highest hopes of Drago Tell Dramis back then, and we haven't changed our minds about his ability. There've been several more interesting incidents since Hera."

"I know," I said. "Seven people died to make this world safe. It would have been well over two hundred if Drago hadn't dreamed up a way to make an incoming group of giant lizards fly over our fuel dump and then blown it up."

"So how do you suggest the situation should be handled?" asked General May.

"Stop pushing the man," I said. "I've had Drago holding the position of a Commander, while only having the rank of Major, for two years. I've resisted several obvious opportunities to promote him. He's nearing thirty now, gaining maturity, and he's got a good team around him. His current deputy has an unusual history, joining the Military when she was slightly older than most recruits, and she's a strong minded, steadying influence."

I paused. "Drago's slowly starting to realize that it's ridiculous he doesn't have the rank to match his position. Give him another Commander's post, let him settle in there for a while, and suffer the embarrassment of a whole new set of officers gossiping about his situation. After that, he should accept being promoted to Commander without too many problems. Once he's made it safely to Commander, he should progress naturally after that. I'm not asking what you have in mind for him in the end, but whatever it is he's at least had time to adjust to the idea."

General May nodded.

"It would be ideal if you could send Drago's team along with Commander Stone to her next posting, because she knows exactly how to handle him."

General May nodded again.

"Of course, it would also help if you could get his father to stop lecturing him," I added, "but I doubt that's humanly possible."

General May laughed. "Thank you, Colonel. It's unfortunate you're retiring. I don't suppose you'd like to…"

"No, sir," I said hastily. "Thank you, but I've considered this very thoroughly. I'm fortunate that I've been able to clear up the final few things that have been worrying me, like Drago's situation, so I can retire in the happy knowledge I'm not leaving any jobs undone."

"Very well," said General May. "I hope you enjoy your retirement."

The call ended, and I turned and went back into the dome. The vid clips were still running. I joined in the laughter at a dozen moments ranging from tense to comical, then the vid sequence ended and the floating suns went to full brightness again.

I had a speech to give, and Drago had thoughtfully put a podium at one end of the dome, so I went to stand on it. This time I'd remembered to wear a microphone. The crowd quietened down and looked expectantly at me.

"As you know, I'm retiring. I don't want to make a tediously long speech that drones on about six decades in the Military, and I've forbidden Commander Stone to make one for me. It's not necessary, because today says it all. Handing over a new world to its first colonists sums up everything that Planet First missions are about. It's been a pleasure serving with so many fine officers. Thank you for helping me to finish my years of service on the highest possible note by adding Maia to the worlds of humanity."

I let them clap for a bit, and then waved at them to quieten down. "And now I have to give you the standard information and warnings before the real party starts. Firstly, this planet is now officially under civilian law. Since the whole of Kappa sector is still using the rules of the Colony Ten charter, you can register Twoing or Threeing contracts yourselves by contacting Kappa Sector Central Registry directly."

I paused. "You can also enter into either a duo or triad marriage without prior notice or previous relationship contracts, but that marriage must be authorized and registered by an appropriate official. As your commanding officer, I qualify as an appropriate official, but Colony Ten rules say I can't authorize marriages for anyone who is even slightly drunk or powered. If you're going to propose to anyone, make sure you do it while all the parties concerned can still pass a blood test!"

Everyone cheered.

"Secondly, the Military must always show respect for variations in cultural attitudes. This dome is the main party zone, and standards of behaviour and dress may not be acceptable to certain officers, particularly those from Delta sector. There is a side dome marked Quiet Zone, with a secondary party area where Delta sector standards will apply. There is a further side dome marked Rest Zone, where those officers without quarters here can go to sleep, and I emphasize the word 'sleep' in that sentence. Other activities should be limited to an officer's private quarters or to the dome marked..."

I broke off and looked round for Drago. "What are you calling that dome this time?"

"It's marked 'The Colonel doesn't want to know,'" yelled Drago.

There was more cheering.

"Right, that's it," I said. "You now have twenty-four hours before the cleanup squad start trying to sober people up and reunite them with their luggage. Have an excellent party, and that's an order!"

I stepped down from the podium, feeling oddly shaky, and went back across to stand with Stone and Leveque. As I reached them, the singing started. Drago's magnified voice alone for the first line, and then the whole mob joining in. Old Lang Zine. A song so old that a lot of the words didn't make sense any longer, but the mere sound of it hit me like an emotional punch in the stomach. Everyone sang it at Year End, as midnight interstellar standard Green Time marked the end of the old year and the start of the new one. The Military sang it at every handover party, as they said goodbye to a world and friends they'd worked with for years and prepared to move on to new challenges.

This time I wasn't moving on. This time there was no new beginning, just old memories. The people around me were hugging each other as they sang, even the enigmatic Leveque had his arm round his wife and was smiling, but I stood alone. People don't randomly hug their commanding officer, but I felt the touch of ghostly arms round my shoulders, and heard the laughter from decades ago.

The last line of the song ended, and there was a moment of silence before a drum beat sounded. Colourful banners started unfurling among the crowd.

"Here we go again," said Nia Stone. "I never know how the Betans can produce their clan banners and drums out of thin air."

I fought off the memories of the past and smiled. It was a standard Military joke that you didn't have to encourage Betans to maintain their cultural heritage, your problem was stopping them!

"Everyone says that Betans have their clan banners surgically implanted at birth," I said.

"I could almost believe that," said Nia Stone.

"The probability of that rumour being true is significantly less than 1 per cent," said Leveque with a perfectly straight face. "Military doctors have consistently failed to find any confirming evidence."

Nia and I laughed.

The array of different clan banners were forming up in the centre of the dome now, surrounded by a mob wearing either Military uniforms or togas. Everyone else moved out of the way and stood watching them.

"I can see the whole of Drago's team out there," said Nia, "though only five of them are Betan."

Leveque shrugged. "Betans have a way of dragging people into things, and Drago's especially good at it."

The clan banners were lined up now, with the banner of Beta sector at the front. Most of the banners were the familiar ones of the Betan Military clans, but there were a few Betans who'd been born into civilian clans, joined the Military as sector recruits, and carried less well-known banners. I saw the flash of a sword among the banners, frowned, and prepared to intervene. Drago should know better than this. The Betans were allowed all the drums and banners they liked at parties, but the use of ceremonial swords was strictly limited to...

The people standing in front of me moved aside, giving me a clearer view of who was holding the sword. I saw it was Captain Marlise Weldon and relaxed. Three years ago, just after graduating the Military Academy, she'd represented the Military in the Olympics at Tai Chi sword form. Her decision to accept Planet First assignments had ended her competitive career, since it meant spending long periods on worlds under strict quarantine, but she still did some training and I knew all her swords had safely blunt blades.

More drums were sounding now, and the beats were faster. I watched Marlise take up the first position of the Tai Chi form, with her sword held vertically behind her. I'd seen her display several times before, but it was always impressive to watch, so I was annoyed when someone came to stand in front of me. I gave them an irritated look and was startled to see it was Drago. He held out a toga towards me.

"Today, you run with us."

I was still emotionally overloaded from the singing, but I clung to sanity. I couldn't go back in time. I couldn't bring the dead to life, and nothing could be the same without them. I shook my head. "I left the clan nearly twenty years ago."

"With respect, you joined the clan on the day of your marriage, and you have never left it. You've just been absent for a while."

I pulled a face. "Drago, I appreciate the gesture, but no."

"Today, you run with us," he repeated.

Drago had obviously planned this carefully, getting Captain Weldon to create a distraction, but the people nearby had started noticing something was going on. Nia Stone was looking puzzled, but Mason Leveque had an unreadable expression on his face. I had a feeling he knew exactly what was happening here. Normal people wouldn't research their commanding officer's personal history from two decades ago, but Leveque was a Threat team leader. It was his job to spot potential dangers, and calculate the best way to deal with them, and the strengths and weaknesses of his commanding officer were an important factor in those calculations. Leveque probably knew the exact date I had my first haircut.

"I said no, Major Tell Dramis." My tone of voice was a sharp order, and now people were openly staring at us.

"This is nothing to do with the Military," said Drago. "This is family. Today, you run with us, Riak." He added something incomprehensible in strong Betan dialect rather than standard Language.

"You're wasting your time talking Betan at me, Drago. I never really got the hang of the dialect."

"What I said was that you're retiring, Riak, and that's a time for returning home. Are you really planning to spend your retirement on a random Military base, sitting listening to other retired officers endlessly repeat the same anecdotes, when you could come home to play a full and active part in the life of your family?"

I couldn't help picturing the clan hall on Zeus, with its constant chaos of serving officers home on leave, civilians, and retired officers. The children too, of course. There was always a crowd of children, left at the clan hall to attend the Military school on Zeus while their parents were on hazardous Planet First assignments. As a retired officer, I'd be expected to help run the clan hall, keep an eye on the children, and offer advice to the teenagers nearing Military recruitment age.

"It could never be the same," I said.

"It could never be the same," said Drago. "But it could be different."

He smiled. It's strange the way a family resemblance can suddenly leap out at you. There was something about Drago's smile...

"Run with us, Riak," said Drago. "If I have to, I'll stand here for hours."

Part IV

Drago thrust the toga at me again, and I found myself taking it. "I'll run with you, Drago, but don't get ideas." I stripped off my jacket, and shrugged the toga on over the top of the rest of my uniform. "I can't just rejoin the clan and move into the clan hall. Not with so many memories of..."

"I understand that," he said. "You could start with a very short visit, and then make some longer ones. Give yourself plenty of time to gradually adjust before moving home permanently."

I tugged my toga roughly into place. There was no point in my trying to adjust the folds properly. However much care I took with it, I knew I'd still look a mess, because I had nearly as much trouble wearing togas as I did wearing Military dress uniforms.

The drum beats had stopped now. I glanced round, saw Marlise Weldon had ended her display, and that everyone in the dome was staring at me and Drago with shocked faces. All except Mason Leveque, who had an odd smile on his face as if he'd expected this to happen.

I turned back to Drago. We hugged each other in the traditional embrace of clan kindred, before taking a step back and solemnly facing each other.

"Fidelis, Riak." Drago saluted me, not with the Military salute, but the right hand on heart salute of Beta sector.

I copied his gesture. I hadn't given a Betan salute for almost two decades, but it seemed oddly natural.

The drums started again, in a staccato rhythm that echoed through my bones and set my pulse beating faster. Drago lifted both arms and turned to face the banners.

"Be-ta!" He separated the two syllables, emphasizing them as if they were different words, and pronouncing the second syllable with the distinctive Betan inflection.

"Be-ta!" The crowd in the centre of the dome answered him.

"Be-ta!" I joined in the chanting.

The Betans started circling the dome at a slow run, parading their banners. Sometimes just one person was with a clan banner, sometimes there were a cluster of people from the same clan. I saw a whole lot of extra people who definitely weren't Betan, including Captain Weldon. She was carrying a heartbreakingly familiar banner.

As the parade reached us, the leader passed the Beta sector banner to Drago, and Captain Weldon held out her banner to me.

I shook my head. "Drago should..."

I looked for Drago, saw he'd already run off leading the parade, and groaned. There wasn't anyone else from our clan here, so I accepted the banner and joined the parade. I was a bit old to be running round a dome waving my clan banner, but Betans have a way of dragging people into things.

By the time we'd circled the dome twice, those of us in the lead had almost caught the ones at the back. One final lap, then the sound of drums reached a climax. There was a burst of wild cheering, the parade stopped, and broke up into groups of laughing people.

The sound of drums was replaced by music now. I gave myself a moment to catch my breath, and then turned to look at the vid display on the far wall. It was blank for a moment, then the names started scrolling up. Mostly in pairs, but occasionally three together. Beside the names were abbreviations to show if it was a standard Twoing or Threeing contract that had been registered, or a request sent to Betan clans to arrange formal betrothal or marriage ceremonies.

Each set of names was greeted by applause and a burst of cheering from somewhere in the dome. This happened at every handover ceremony. Some relationships would have been agreed months ago, but the people involved had deliberately waited for this moment to register a contract with their friends around them. Others would have made a spur of the moment decision, hit by emotion during the singing of Old Lang Zine, and the knowledge that this was their last chance.

Tomorrow, all the thousands of people here would head off on leave, scattering across hundreds of different worlds. After that statutory leave, they'd move on to random new assignments. Any sort of formal commitment, even the minimum three month Twoing contract, guaranteed your next assignment would be together. Without one, you'd probably spend the next few years apart.

So some of the relationships scrolling up the wall were serious commitments. Others were just to give a casual attraction a chance to turn into something more. They all got their cheers though. The list finally reached the end, only to suddenly jerk on again as a couple of extremely last minute decisions were made.

I retrieved my jacket, turned on my microphone and called out. "Attention everyone. Marriage time! Anyone wanting to get married should see the Medical team leader for their blood tests, and then come down to join me in the Quiet Zone."

I headed off down the corridor that linked this dome to the next one, went past a large notice that said "You are entering the Quiet Zone! Betans Put Your Clothes On!", and followed an arrow marked "Marriages" down a side corridor to a small meeting room.

I dumped my jacket on the back of a chair, sat down at the circular table, and buried my face in my hands. What had come over me back there? Wearing a toga again! Embracing Drago as my clan kindred! Carrying the clan banner! What the chaos did the people watching think?

And a female voice in my head spoke. "It doesn't matter what anyone thinks. We are Betan, and we are proud of it!"

There was male laughter. "You're back with us at last, farm boy. What took you so long?"

"Don't sound so sickeningly smug about it!" I said aloud. "You've no idea how bad it was to be the one left alive and struggling with survivor guilt. I still think I'm making a huge mistake. I've more or less committed myself to visit the clan hall, and going there could never be the same."

The female voice in my head spoke. "But it could be different."

I sighed. "That's what Drago said. He's got your smile, you know. That's what made me..."

There was a chime from the door. I hastily stopped talking to myself, and tapped the control on the table. The door opened and a man and woman entered. Their faces were familiar, but I'd forgotten their names. Thousands of officers had worked on Maia, so it wasn't surprising I couldn't remember them all.

I checked the messages on my lookup and found their marriage request. They were two of the Military scientists, which meant I'd had less contact with them than the combat Military officers. Both in their early twenties, both born in Delta sector, and the medical check showed they were perfectly sober. I had absolutely nothing to worry about here.

I smiled at them. "I see you've got five prior Twoing contracts, which means you could register your marriage conventionally as soon as you're on leave back in Delta sector."

"We felt it was more appropriate now," said the man. "This is an emotional day."

I nodded, took their handprints, registered the marriage, and gave them my congratulations. The next couple were two women who I definitely recognized. I frowned at them.

"I married you two last year! Is this some sort of anniversary re-enactment?"

They exchanged embarrassed looks. "Our divorce was finalized an hour ago," said one of them.

"We decided it was a mistake," said the other.

I remembered the conversation between Stone and Leveque just before the handover ceremony. Presumably they'd been talking about these two. "You're quite sure you want to get married again? I've got several more marriage requests, so you could go to the back of the queue and take a few more minutes to think about it."

"We're sure," said one of them.

"It was my fault," said the other. "I should have told her about..."

I lifted a hand to stop her. "I'm not asking for private details. I just want to know you've thought carefully about this."

"We have," they chorused.

I did the registering and congratulations routine. The next ten marriages were straightforward. All established couples from Military families. All duo marriages. I'd very rarely had to officiate at a triad marriage in my career, because most of them involved at least one Betan, and Betans always wanted proper clan ceremonies.

The last but one couple puzzled me. They were another two of the Military scientists, but I remembered this pair perfectly. I'd had to give them disciplinary lectures at least four times because their running feud with each other was disrupting their work.

"I thought you two hated each other."

The man shrugged. The woman nodded. "We do."

"Why do you want to get married if you hate each other?"

They both started speaking at once, and broke off to glare at each other. "I don't believe that information is relevant," said the man.

"I think it is." I quoted Military Regulations. "When officiating at a marriage, a commanding officer must ensure all parties have given due thought to the commitment involved."

"It's a purely temporary arrangement," said the man. "We've been informed we're a genetically desirable match, and we want the child to be born within a marriage for legal reasons."

I gave him a startled look, and hastily checked their records. Both born on Freya in Alpha sector, and obviously believers in its old genetically-guided parenthood system. Under the rules of the Military Charter, my official actions had to be politically neutral and without prejudice. Whatever my personal opinions, I had no right to refuse to marry these people.

I sighed, went through the formalities, offered congratulations that didn't seem very welcome, and gloomily watched the pair of them leave.

The final couple on the marriage list were a total contrast. Two lieutenants, both from Military families, who'd arrived from the Military Academy just three months ago. They looked incredibly young, but everyone under the age of 40 looked young to me these days. The way they were holding on to each other told me they were genuinely in love, so I was far happier marrying them than the couple from Freya who hated each other.

When they'd left, I frowned down at the table. I'd planned to rejoin the party at this point, but only stay long enough to say a personal farewell to a few key people before going back to my quarters to finish my packing. After that, my idea had been to quietly leave for Tethys in Gamma sector. I hadn't been back to my home world since my parents died, and I had an odd hankering for a nostalgic visit to the carrot fields.

Things were different now though. The wall shielding me from the past was breaking down, so I had to rethink everything. I ran my fingers through my hair. I'd stay for most of the party, and then go to Tethys as planned, but a couple of days with the carrots should be more than enough to rekindle my old hatred of them. After that, I'd go to Zeus in Beta sector, and revisit a few places I hadn't seen in two decades, like Lake Galad. If I coped with that, then maybe I'd call in at the clan hall for an hour.

I heard the female voice in my head. "Why did you two decide on Galad as the male surname for our triad marriage?"

"We've told you that at least a dozen times," said the male voice in my head. "Combining Torrek with my surname came out sounding silly. Riak and I went on a boat trip at Lake Galad just before our betrothal ceremony. That was when we talked through his concerns about exactly how the relationships in our triad marriage would work."

There was a female sigh. "I still have the feeling you're hiding something."

She was right. What actually happened was we were messing about and capsized our boat. He scared me to death by vanishing underwater, and I dived down to save him from a watery grave, only to discover the man could swim like a fish and was happily trying to retrieve his jacket from the lake bed.

Once we reached the beach, he made the mistake of teasing me about my panic-stricken reaction to his assumed death by drowning. I was in an emotionally unstable state, so I hit him over the head with a beach parasol, and the fight ended with us both getting arrested. The conversation about relationships took place when we were locked in neighbouring prison cells.

Betan dialect has a lot of different words to describe the possible triad relationships. There is one where two of the partners have a deep platonic love for each other. There is another where two of the partners have a deep platonic hatred for each other. We established that we had our own subtle mixture of these, since he was happy to admit we were the first, but I felt more comfortable pretending we were the second. However much he might enjoy teasing me about that, and trying to push me into admitting the truth, he'd better not overdo it or I'd hit him over the head with another beach parasol.

On any planet outside Beta sector, the civilian authorities would have handed the pair of us over to Military Security, and we'd have been put on report for public brawling. We were on Zeus though, so an official eventually turned up, and got us to state we were both willing participants in the fight. After that, we just had to pay for the beach parasol I'd broken and we were free to leave.

A chime from my lookup interrupted my thoughts. I glanced down at it, saw Marack was calling me, accepted the call and projected his holo image in midair. I frowned when I saw the state he was in. His uniform was crumpled, he looked exhausted, the age lines on his face were deeper than usual, and there was a spectacular bruise on his forehead. His grim expression changed to shock as he saw me.

"You're wearing a toga, Father!"

I'd totally forgotten I was still wearing the toga. "You can blame Drago for that. He practically forced me into it. Never mind that now. What's been happening on K19448? You look as if you haven't slept in a week."

"I certainly haven't slept in days," said Marack. "It looked as if we had the planet stable, but everything suddenly exploded again. You know how fast trouble can flare up on Planet First missions."

I nodded.

"That's why I'm calling you," said Marack. "My replacement was supposed to arrive next week. I was going to spend a few days handing things over to him, then head to Alpha sector and take up my new post commanding the five Earth solar arrays."

"You don't think you'll be able to leave?" I asked.

"I know I won't be able to leave," said Marack. "We've just had to send K19448 back to maximum quarantine status."

"Chaos!" I knew how desperately Marack wanted that post commanding the Earth solar arrays. "That means you can only leave if K19448 has a full emergency evacuation, and even then you'll be stuck in a quarantine area for ages."

"I need to get to Earth within the next two weeks to take up my new command," said Marack, "and I can't possibly make it. Solar Array Command can't hold the position for me, because they know this sort of Planet First situation is totally unpredictable. I could be stuck here for months, even years, so they'll have to appoint someone else. I hate to ask this, Father, but..."

"Yes," I interrupted him. "Of course I'll take the position until you arrive, and then hand it over to you. At least, I will if I'm eligible for it. I'm no expert on the technical side of running solar arrays."

"You leave the technical side to your Science team leader," said Marack. "Your job is managing people and making any necessary command decisions."

He paused. "It would be a huge relief to me if you do this, Father. General Dragon Tell Dramis has offered to be a temporary substitute for me, which is extremely generous of him, but you know the reason I'm so eager to get this Earth posting and Dragon..."

He didn't need to finish his sentence, because I was already shuddering at the idea. "Oh no, we can't let Dragon go anywhere near this! He's brilliant at wading into lethally dangerous situations and getting them under control, but when it comes to dealing with people he has all the sensitivity of a charging herd of Asgard bison. I know that the second Dragon hears I've been seen in public wearing a toga, he'll be pushing me to rejoin the clan, allocating me rooms in the clan hall, and suggesting duties I can perform."

I pulled a face. "I know Dragon would only be doing those things because he wants to welcome me back to the family, but rejoining the clan is a huge emotional journey for me. I need to take it at my own speed, or I'll fall apart all over again."

"You mustn't let Dragon put you off returning home to us," said Marack.

"I won't." I smiled. "Dragon's fond of giving other people lectures, but if he starts pushing me to do things I'm not ready for, I'll be the one giving him the lecture for a change."

Marack laughed. "Dragon won't like that."

"He'll hate it, but my age means he'll just have to listen in dutiful silence. Dragon may be a General, and on clan council, but he still has to treat his elderly uncle with proper respect."

I paused. "Anyway, my point is that I'll make sure Dragon doesn't interfere with my return to the clan, because I know his idea of being helpful could destroy everything for me. I'll make sure that he stays away from Earth as well, because I don't want him destroying things for you either. Is there anyone specific I should contact about this assignment?"

Marack shook his head.

"Then I'll call General Kpossi at Colony Ten Command. She's been trying to talk me into taking another post, so she should be happy to help me with this. Colony Ten Command need to be constantly operational, so they run shifts, and I'm not sure what General Kpossi's shift pattern is. It may take me a while to get to talk to her, so leave this with me while you try and get some sleep."

Marack groaned. "My problem won't be getting to sleep, but waking up again. K19448 has a twenty-four hour and sixteen minutes long day and I could sleep for all of it."

I laughed. "Go ahead and do that. When you wake up, you'll hopefully find a message from me telling you that everything's arranged. Now I'm saying goodbye, so you go to bed and sleep!"

I ended that call, shrugged off my toga, put my uniform jacket back on, and made another call to Colony Ten Command. I wasn't sure whether to go via their Command Support or contact General Kpossi directly, but compromised by sending General Kpossi a text message, flagged as non-urgent, asking her to contact me when convenient about a possible posting. I was pleased to get an almost instant response, but rather confused by the misty image on my lookup screen.

The mist abruptly cleared, and I saw General Kpossi's face, her hair trailing limply round it and dripping water. "What position have you found to tempt you, Colonel?" she asked.

"The command of the Earth solar arrays, sir. Their future commanding officer will be late taking it up because of a Planet First problem. I'd like to take the position as a temporary measure until he arrives."

The image on my lookup screen went misty again, and I realized the lookup was underwater. A moment later, it cleared. There were a series of random glimpses of a swimming pool, followed by a close-up view of a towel. General Kpossi obviously wore her lookup and continued working while swimming.

The towel vanished from view, and then appeared again, this time wrapped round General Kpossi's head. "I'd prefer you to take another permanent position, Colonel, but a temporary one is a good start. I'll give Solar Array Command a call right now and set that up for you."

"Thank you, sir."

I ended the call. I'd just sent the promised message to Marack, when there was a chime from the door. I gave it a bewildered look, tapped the table top, and the door opened. Leveque and Stone came in.

"The last of the married couples rejoined the party ages ago, sir," said Stone. "We were getting worried you'd sneaked away without saying goodbye."

"Actually, I've been busy arranging a new posting," I said.

Leveque gave me a startled look. Judging from his expression, my Threat team leader had calculated the chances of me accepting another post as virtually zero.

I smiled. "Don't worry, Mason. Your predictive skills haven't let you down. I'm not giving up the idea of retiring, just taking a temporary post to help out my son, Marack."

"Would you need a deputy commander and a Threat team leader on this posting?" asked Leveque.

I shook my head. "If this was another Planet First posting, then I'd be calling on you two and a lot of the other people from this command to go with me, but it's not. I'll be having a dreadfully boring time commanding the Earth solar arrays, where the biggest excitement is likely to be the food dispensers running out of Fizzup."

I picked up my toga and shrugged it on. "Let's get back to the party!"

ZETA SECTOR 2788 - MAJOR DRAGO TELL DRAMIS

Zeus, Beta Sector, October 2788. Readers voted on which character they'd like me to feature in the final story for this collection, and they chose Major Drago Tell Dramis, a character who doesn't appear in the Earth Girl trilogy until the second book, Earth Star. Drago also appears in Kappa Sector 2788, and this story is set immediately after that story ends.

Part I

Technically speaking, I was born an Alphan, because I let out my first outraged baby wails in the Medical Centre at Military Headquarters on the planet Academy in Alpha sector. Far more importantly though, I was born a member of one of the famous Military clans of Beta sector. The Tell clan hall on the Betan capital planet, Zeus, was the one stable point in my twenty-eight nomad years as first a Military child and then a Military officer. Despite my dual Alphan and Betan citizenship, my heart was wholly Betan, and I counted Zeus as my true home world.

Returning to Zeus after a long Military assignment was always a little nerve-wracking. I could count on our clan hall being comfortingly unchanged, because it was a clan policy to stick to classic furnishings and decor rather than follow the rapidly changing fashions of Zeus. The rest of the planet was much less considerate during my absences, so I never knew which of my old haunts I'd find had altered beyond recognition, or even vanished entirely.

I held my breath as I walked into Asante's MeetUp, then relaxed as I saw the familiar marble pillars, and the gloriously fake, luxuriant grape vines growing up the walls. I scanned the crowded room slowly, recognizing some old friends of mine, like the aging, silver-haired Constantine who was as fixed a part of this place as the marble pillars.

I was really looking for the bartender, Asante, of course. On frontier worlds, a bartender wore functional clothes, stood behind a bar and served drinks. Here on Zeus, a bartender traditionally wore a flamboyant version of a laurel wreath, and roamed the room playing the role of welcoming host, while the drinks came from automated dispensers. Beta sector prided itself on being inspired by ancient Rome, and wearing laurel wreaths was somehow supposed to link bartenders with Bacchus, the ancient Roman god of wine and revelry.

I finally spotted Asante's ludicrous laurel wreath at the far end of the room. He'd made a few alterations to it since the last time I was here. It was coloured imperial purple now, with matching tiny purple lights that flashed brightly among the black twisted strands of his hair. I raised an eyebrow when I realized Asante was sitting on an ornate throne on a raised dais. I could see a throne would serve the twin function of indulging his colossal ego, while also giving him a good view of everything happening in the room, but a throne still seemed a little ostentatious even for Asante.

My Military uniform made me conspicuous among the people in party clothes, so Asante spotted me at the same moment that I saw him. He gave me one of his improbably wide smiles, which always made me wonder if his face would split in half one day, jumped down from his throne, and hurried over to meet me.

"Attention everyone, the irresistible Drago Tell Dramis is back among us!" he shouted in his deep, booming voice. He was using Betan dialect rather than standard Language. As a fiercely loyal Betan, Asante refused to speak the common tongue of humanity on principle, and constantly complained about Betan schools and newzie channels being forced to use it.

There was a round of applause and appreciative whistles as people got up from their seats and came to gather round us. I felt myself blush.

"*Finally* back among us," added Asante pointedly.

I laughed and replied in Betan dialect myself, having to think carefully about which words were the same as in Language and which were radically different. I always had a problem when I first came home after spending a long time almost exclusively speaking Language. My brain seemed to need a couple of days to shake the dust off the part of itself that could automatically switch between Betan dialect and Language.

"I warned you I was going on what would probably be a long Planet First assignment," I said. "When the Military are making a new world safe for humanity, we have to work under strict quarantine restrictions, so officers can't casually portal home on leave."

"Yes, but I didn't expect it to be two whole years before I saw you again," said Asante. "I was beginning to think you'd turned traitor and found yourself a different MeetUp on Zeus."

"You should know I'm your faithful subject." I knelt on one knee, and gave him the ancient right hand on heart salute of Beta sector. "Hail, Asante!"

"Oh no," called Constantine. "Don't start kneeling to him, Drago. We don't want a repeat of last year."

I got back to my feet. "What happened last year?"

Constantine smiled. "Asante decided Beta sector should declare its independence as the Third Roman Empire, with himself as Emperor. You must have noticed his new imperial laurel wreath and throne."

The whole room erupted in laughter and reminiscent jokes, but I frowned, hit by multiple conflicting emotions. The part of me that was loyal to Beta sector was proud of the time nearly two centuries ago, when Beta sector had declared the second Roman Empire under Emperor Haran Augustus, and had stood alone and defiant against the rest of humanity.

But the part of me loyal to the Military took a very different view. For the fifty-three year duration of the Second Roman Empire, humanity had hovered on the brink of war between the sectors. It had been a dreadful time for the Military, with officers who'd joined up to defend humanity from danger having to face the possibility of using their weapons against fellow human beings.

And the part of me that was loyal to my clan shuddered at the mere mention of the Second Roman Empire. That time had been an utter nightmare for the members of the sprawling extended families of the Military clans of Beta sector. I'd seen the vids in my clan archives, showing my ancestors having anguished clan meetings, torn between their oaths as Betans and as Military. After seeing those vids, the thought of Beta sector declaring the Third Roman Empire, of finding myself in exactly the same position, was far from funny.

"Asante took everyone over to the Parthenon," continued Constantine, "so we could hear him make a speech to Senate, ordering them to defend Betan clan culture and sexual freedom by attacking Gamma sector."

There was another burst of laughter, and I forced myself to smile. The people around me were civilians, and couldn't possibly understand how I felt about this. They thought there was a big gulf between the culture of Beta and the other sectors, but they didn't realize there was a far bigger division between Military and civilian life.

Since over 90 per cent of Military recruits had been born into Military families themselves, and grown up either on Military bases or in Betan Military clan halls, few civilians even knew one of us personally, let alone understood the life we lived. The Military did all the dangerous jobs of humanity, preparing new colony worlds to be safe homes for people, and going in as a peacekeeping force on worlds where planetary political arguments threatened to escalate into civil war. We did our job well, perhaps too well. Civilians led a protected, sheltered existence, and could expect to live to celebrate their hundredth. They had no idea of the true horror of death and conflict.

On Remembrance Day each year, civilians would spare a few moments to solemnly remember the Military who'd died protecting them, but they got their ideas of those deaths from naively romantic entertainment vids. They pictured them all as happening in heroic circumstances, with the bodies looking dignified and nobly peaceful in death, just like the statues at a memorial site. They'd never seen a friend die in a stupidly pointless accident, or had to respectfully gather together the pieces of what had been their body for burial.

If something happened to me one day, then the lives of the people who knew me at Asante's MeetUp might be briefly touched by shadow, but I'd soon become a nostalgic memory. They'd never face danger themselves. They'd never know the intense moment when you were hit by the reality that doing something could kill you, but you did it anyway, because you were Military and never wanted to be anything else.

It was the job of the Military to protect civilians from such grim realities, not to spoil a happy moment with lectures about wars being an inappropriate subject for jokes. I did my best to speak in a light-hearted voice. "How did the members of Senate react to Asante's arrival?"

Hermione and Nyakeo, Asante's wives, came out from the crowd. Hermione had had blonde hair trailing loose past her shoulders last time I saw her, but now her hair was red and caught up in an ornate knot on top of her head. Nyakeo looked the same as ever though, hair and skin as dark as Asante, and with an infectiously happy grin on her face.

They both kissed me on the cheek, and then Hermione spoke. "It was nearly midnight, so the whole of Senate had gone home hours ago, but the Praetorian Honour Guard were still guarding the building. They were very friendly and helpful when we explained what was happening. They let Asante stand on the steps, declare himself Emperor, and make his speech. They even saluted him at the end."

"I made a vid of the whole thing," added Nyakeo, "and they used a clip on Beta Sector Daily. I'll send you a copy if you like, Drago. It's a shame you weren't there to be in the vid yourself."

I pictured myself in Military uniform, joining the Praetorian Honour Guard in saluting Emperor Asante, and cringed. The Praetorian Honour Guard was made up of bodyguards employed by the Betan Senate, and encouraged to entertain the public, while I was a genuine Military officer. All the newzie channels would have grabbed the chance to show the vid clip, and Military Command...

Actually, however strongly Military Command disapproved, they couldn't have done much to me, because celebrating my cultural heritage was specifically permitted under Military Regulations. They wouldn't have needed to do anything anyway, because Father would have shot me. If Mother was around at the time, she'd have stopped him of course, but then I'd have had to suffer a lifetime of endless lectures about my irresponsible behaviour. On the whole, I'd have been better off being shot.

In reality though, none of those things would have happened. I wasn't nearly as immature and reckless as my father imagined. However much I adored encouraging the delightful eccentricities of Asante inside his MeetUp, I'd have had to disappoint him by refusing to take part in a public display. It was fortunate that his acclamation as Emperor had happened while I was away on assignment.

One thing about this story puzzled me. Asante's hostility to other sectors was normally centred on privileged Alpha sector, the traditional rival of Beta sector, so... "Why did you want to attack Gamma sector in particular?"

Asante gave a dramatic wave of his right hand. "When Alpha and Gamma sectors united to try and impose their cultural standards on Beta sector back in 2605, we defied them. We will do the same again now in 2788. Fidelis!"

"Fidelis!" yelled the mob.

I frowned. "I know I don't have access to the full range of Betan newzie channels when I'm on a nameless prospective colony world in Kappa sector, but if we were facing a political situation like there was in 2605 then every newzie channel in every sector would be screaming about it."

"I admit it was on a much smaller scale," said Asante, "but the principle was the same."

"What actually happened was a minor Gamma sector politician made a speech condemning the immorality of Beta sector," said Hermione. "Apparently, he'd been part of some official Gamma sector delegation that came to Zeus. He went into a MeetUp like this one and didn't like what he saw."

She paused and adopted a prim, masculine tone of voice, before quoting what I guessed was part of the speech. "I'm a tolerant man. I accept that triad marriage is legal in Beta sector, I accept the peculiarities of their clan system and their mangled interpretation of ancient Roman and Greek culture, but I cannot accept the way they scandalize innocent visitors to their worlds with their immoral clothing standards. I was shocked, appalled, and outraged to see women brazenly flaunting their naked fronts at me!"

Constantine grinned. "Beta sector's official response was to ban him from ever visiting a Betan world again. The message said we couldn't guarantee that every single one of the tens of billions of people in Beta sector would remain suitably dressed at all times just in case he walked through their door, and didn't want any risk of him suffering such alarming shock and distress again. Asante's demonstration was one of a host of unofficial responses, including the new fashion in party clothes. You must have noticed our clothes."

Naturally I'd noticed everyone was wearing glittering, jewel-coloured clothes, which covered an oddly large amount of the body for Beta sector. It wasn't exactly true that Betans had no nudity taboo, and there were plenty of places and occasions where full formal dress including a toga was expected, but there was usually a lot more skin on display in a MeetUp, particularly Asante's MeetUp.

"I was a bit puzzled by the clothes," I said.

Asante gave one of his widest smiles. "Gamma sector would like us to wear clothes that cover the body areas they consider private, so we are. The clothes are slightly different to the ones in Gamma sector though, because they're made with cutaway cloth sections. Watch what happens when people dance."

He clapped his hands. "Bar command slow dance music!"

Music started playing from the overhead speakers, and people began swaying from side to side. As they moved, unexpected flashes of bare skin kept appearing.

"Drago, do you think my dress would impress the men of Gamma sector?" called a beautiful, raven-haired girl.

I turned to look at her, and she deliberately span round on the spot. Every cutaway on her sapphire-blue outfit triggered at once, so for a second or two she was only wearing flying lengths of blue ribbon. Everyone applauded her.

I choked. "I think it would have a devastating effect on them."

She grinned at me. "And how about you, Drago? Does it have a devastating effect on you?"

Betan courtesy demanded I give her a deeply appreciative smile and a compliment. "The lovely dress, and the display of its even lovelier contents, has so utterly devastated me that I need a glass of wine to help me recover. May your humble subject offer you wine as an apology for his overlong absence, Asante?"

"I shall have a glass of wine from Aether," said Asante.

We went across to the nearest drinks dispenser, I ordered two glasses of the distinctive, sharp-tasting, red wine from Aether, and we took the drinks to a small table in the corner and sat down. The rest of the crowd accepted the current entertainment was over, and drifted back to sit at their own tables and resume their interrupted conversations.

Asante studied me for a moment before speaking. "Why are you buying me wine, Drago? You should be eagerly pursuing the enchanting Clarinda after that charming invitation she gave you."

"Clarinda is the girl in blue? She must be new here, because I've never seen her before."

"Relatively new," said Asante. "She's been coming to my MeetUp for a year now, so she's heard all about the irresistible Drago Tell Dramis. She seems eager to be your partner while you're here on leave, and you'd have a lot of fun together."

"I'm sure we would, but I'm not interested in tumbling a girl who must be ten years younger than me."

"If I remember correctly, Drago, you're 28," said Asante.

I nodded.

"And Clarinda is 22 not 18."

I shrugged. "She looks younger."

"She's very attractive."

"She's stunning, but I'm still not interested." I paused. "The truth is that I've fallen in love, Asante."

"Ah ha!" He leaned back in his chair. "So you bought me wine because you wanted to tell me about your lover. Does he, she, or they have a name?"

"Her name is Marlise, and I need you to advise me what to do about her."

Asante frowned. "I'd have thought it was obvious what you should do. I know you've enjoyed your years of freedom and exploring casual relationships, Drago, but you're 28 now. It's time for you to start thinking seriously about settling down into a permanent relationship. The look on your face shows you're besotted with this girl, so why not marry her?"

I groaned. "Please don't start preaching to me about Betans traditionally settling down and marrying by 30, Asante. I've been having that lecture from my father at least once a month for the last three years, and anyway it's not needed. I want to marry Marlise, but we've been nothing more than friends so far, and I'm scared to push things between us."

"What?" Asante dramatically hit his forehead with his right hand, and his laurel wreath nearly fell off. "The irresistible Drago Tell Dramis is a Military hero, smothered with medals, and never scared of anything."

"I'm not just scared, I'm petrified," I said. "If I ask Marlise to marry me, and she turns me down, then..."

Asante sighed. "I don't understand what's going on here, Drago. You're irresistibly handsome, and I've seen you charm a girl into tumbling you in less than two minutes, so why are you panicking that your Marlise will turn you down?"

"Because Marlise doesn't seem to find me irresistible, and because..." I glanced round to make sure that nobody was lurking close enough to hear what I was saying. "Because the last time I asked someone to marry me, they didn't just turn me down, they laughed in my face."

Part II

I looked at Asante's startled expression. "I'd better get us some more glasses of wine before I tell you about that."

"You'd better get us a bottle," said Asante. "This could be a very long conversation. You've never mentioned a failed marriage proposal before."

"It's not something I enjoy talking about."

"Then why tell me?"

"I told you, I need your advice. I trust your judgement on relationships more than anyone else I know, but you'll never understand why I'm so scared about pursuing things with Marlise unless I tell you about Gemelle."

I went over to the drinks dispenser, got a bottle of wine, and topped up our glasses before sitting down again. "Do you remember meeting my cousin, Jaxon? He's Military too, and nearly two years older than me."

Asante nodded. "You've brought him here four or five times over the years."

"Gemelle is his younger sister. She and I are close enough in age that we ended up in the same class at the Military Academy. Up until then, she'd just been a cousin that I met occasionally at the clan hall, but at the Academy we were spending almost every waking hour together. We became close friends, and eventually I realized I was in love with her, but there was a big problem."

"Was the genetic link between you too close?" asked Asante.

I shook my head. There were Betan dialect words to describe every possible genetic relationship, but after barely speaking dialect for two years, I couldn't remember the right one. I explained it the long way instead.

"Gemelle's grandmother and my grandfather were brother and sister, so a relationship between us was perfectly legal. The problem was that Gemelle was already involved with a boy in the same class as us. I'm afraid that didn't worry me to start with. Back then I really did think I was irresistible. I was certain I could steal Gemelle from him, and I didn't care how he'd feel about it."

I paused to pull a face of self-loathing. "I was a horribly selfish boy, so I didn't spare the slightest thought for anyone's feelings but my own. I had a routine of casually using my looks and my smile like weapons to make girls fall for me, so I smirked at Gemelle and expected her to swoon at my feet."

"But she didn't?" asked Asante.

"No, she told me that she was in what she believed could become a long-term serious relationship, and I should find another girl to tumble."

I gulped down a mouthful of wine. "This is where it starts getting really bad. I'd never been rejected before, and I couldn't believe Gemelle really preferred someone else to me. I pestered her for a few months, thinking she was bound to change her mind, but she didn't. My ego still couldn't believe she didn't want me, so I came up with the theory that she was only staying with her boyfriend because he'd convinced her he wanted a serious relationship. We were nearing graduation, so I was getting increasingly desperate. I decided I had to prove I wanted a serious relationship too, and tried to... outbid the boyfriend by proposing marriage to Gemelle."

Asante blinked. "Wasn't proposing marriage a little drastic in those circumstances?"

"It wasn't just drastic, it was ridiculous," I said. "Looking back at it now, I can understand why Gemelle's reaction was to laugh at me. She was totally happy with her current relationship, but this ridiculously egotistical boy thought he only had to say the word and she'd dump her boyfriend and marry him. Back then, though, I was shocked and angry to be laughed at like that. I was used to getting my own way all the time and..."

I groaned. "I was a truly disgusting person back then. I'm deeply ashamed of what I did next. I hope I've changed and would never act like that again, but I can't forget..."

Asante frowned. "What the chaos did you do next, Drago?"

"I set things up so Gemelle thought her boyfriend was cheating on her. My plan was to split them up, so Gemelle would get together with me instead. The first part of the plan worked but the second didn't. Gemelle dumped her boyfriend, but she still wasn't interested in me, and she was obviously really distressed about what had happened."

I was silent for a moment. "That was when it finally started occurring to me that I wasn't the centre of humanity's space. Other people weren't toys for me to play with or toss aside at my whim, but human beings with feelings and rights. I sat down and thought hard about what I'd done to Gemelle, and how I'd feel if someone had done that to me. I decided I had to try and put things right, so I went and told her the truth."

"What did Gemelle say to that?" asked Asante.

"She didn't say a word. She just broke my nose, then stalked off to talk to her ex-boyfriend. Unfortunately, my broken nose was easier to fix than their broken relationship. When we graduated from the Military Academy, the boyfriend was still refusing to forgive Gemelle, which meant she wouldn't forgive me."

I pulled a face. "I'd made a total mess of everything for both of us. On our last day at the Academy, I tried talking to the boyfriend myself. That didn't help, and Gemelle thought I'd been trying to cause yet more trouble. When we came home to the clan hall on leave, she did everything she could to avoid me, even pointedly walking out of the dining hall when I accidentally sat at the same table as her."

"Disagreements between clan members cause trouble for the whole clan," said Asante. "I'm surprised your clan council didn't talk to you both about it."

"They did," I said grimly. "I admitted everything was my fault. Gemelle was generous enough not to say exactly what I'd done, and fortunately clan council didn't insist on hearing the details. We agreed that I'd stay away from Gemelle whenever possible, and she wouldn't cause a scene when we were forced to be together by something like a clan gathering."

"She never got back together with the boyfriend?" asked Asante.

"No." I sighed. "Gemelle finally started seeing someone else, and things have improved between us to the point where we have brief and awkwardly polite conversations at clan gatherings, but she still doesn't trust me. When she got married, she made me swear never to talk to her husband except when she was with him."

I paused. "Only Jaxon ever heard the full story of what happened between me and Gemelle. My first posting after leaving the Military Academy was as a member of his fighter team. Gemelle stopped visiting him, because she didn't want to risk meeting me. He thought she was over-reacting to some trivial disagreement, so I had to tell him everything."

"What did he think about it?"

"I thought for a moment that he'd break my nose too, but he didn't. Of course he was my team leader at the time, which limited his options. The Military doesn't approve of its officers fighting, and Military Regulations are especially forceful about not punching officers who are directly under your command. As it turned out, Jaxon had done something himself that he deeply regretted. Like me, he'd never been able to make things right. We ended up getting drunk, and making some extremely incoherent vows about becoming better people and putting the happiness of others ahead of our own."

We sat in silence for a while. "Have you made a decision yet?" I asked at last.

"About what?" asked Asante.

"Whether I'm allowed to keep coming to your MeetUp after what I did. I know you have strict standards on behaviour."

"I don't allow troublemakers in my MeetUp," said Asante. "If I ever see the boy you've described in here, then I'll throw him out, but I don't think he exists any longer. You've been coming to my MeetUp for eight years, you've never tried to push your company on anyone, never been ungracious turning down unwelcome advances, and never made anyone unhappy."

He picked up the bottle and poured more wine into our glasses. "You're telling me that your last marriage proposal was a total disaster, so now you're scared to propose marriage to your Marlise in case it ends just as badly."

"Exactly. People constantly tease me, saying I'm irresistible, but the truth is that after my disaster with Gemelle I stopped taking risks. I don't chase after anyone who hasn't already offered me an unmistakeable invitation, like Clarinda did earlier, so I'm never turned down. I don't have a relationship that lasts for longer than a few weeks, so it can't develop into anything serious. I don't get emotionally involved, so I can't get hurt."

I paused. "The situation with Marlise is different in every way. She hasn't given me the faintest sign she's interested in me. We've been friends for over a year. I'm already emotionally involved."

Asante thought for a moment. "Even if you proposed and Marlise turned you down, it couldn't possibly cause as much trouble as last time. Marlise isn't a member of your clan, is she?"

Marlise wasn't a member of my clan, she wasn't even Betan, but she was Military which was what really mattered.

Sometimes marriage with a civilian could work, my own mother was a civilian, but part of my attraction to Marlise came from our shared love of the Military life.

Given Asante's views on people from other sectors, I thought I'd better not mention that Marlise wasn't Betan. I wanted him advising me on how best to court Marlise, not trying to talk me into accepting Clarinda's invitation instead.

"No," I said, "Marlise isn't a clan member, but making a mess of things with her would still cause a lot of trouble. I'm the leader of a fighter team, and Marlise is my deputy. If we're on bad terms, it's not just awkward for everyone in the team, but positively dangerous. We wouldn't be getting lectures from clan council but from our commanding officer, and one of us would probably have to be reassigned."

I shook my head. "What happened with Gemelle was dreadful enough, but the idea of Marlise hating me and leaving my team is hideous. I'd have lost someone who's very important to me as both a deputy and a friend."

"But you won't be making a mess of things this time. You aren't the same person now, Drago. You're older and wiser, and Marlise doesn't have a boyfriend." Asante gave me a questioning look. "Or does she?"

"She did when she first joined my team to replace my previous deputy, but she decided to end that relationship a few months later. I swear that was absolutely nothing to do with me." I lifted both hands to proclaim my innocence. "Once I was sure the relationship was over, I tried hinting that I'd like us to be more than friends, but Marlise just told me not to play my Betan flirting games with her."

"So you gave up?" Asante shook his head in disbelief.

"I didn't give up exactly. Planet K21228 was nearly ready to be handed over to its first colonists, so I decided that the safest thing would be to wait until the handover party before doing anything drastic. When the Military hand over a new world to its first colonists, there's a big party for all the officers who've helped made the world safe, with a point at the start of the party where people traditionally propose to each other. I thought it would be much easier for me to say something then, and if Marlise rejected me then the whole team would be going on leave for months. That would give Marlise and me time to sort things out between us, and get back to being friends, before we were all together again."

"So what happened at this party?" asked Asante. "Did you propose, or just ask her to tumble you?"

"I sort of proposed."

"You sort of proposed?" Asante waved both hands. "What does that mean?"

"I was trying to be a little... ambiguous about it. I thought if Marlise didn't like the idea, then it would make life easier if we could pretend I hadn't really been talking about marriage but friendship. Anyway, Marlise stared at me and asked how much I'd had to drink to make me turn so sentimental. I still can't work out if she realized I was talking about marriage at all."

I shrugged. "At the end of the party, everyone headed off on leave, and I came to beg you for your expert advice, Asante."

He poured the last of the wine into our glasses, picked up the empty bottle, and put it on the metal disc in the centre of the table. "Furniture command table cleanup."

The metal disc obediently swivelled aside, letting the bottle drop into the cleanser chute below. A mechanical arm extended to wipe the table with a cloth, before the metal disc closed again. Traditionally, tables made a noise to indicate that cleanup was complete. In Asante's MeetUp, the noise was a loud, self-satisfied burp.

"What is Marlise like?" asked Asante.

"She's incredible." I grinned. "I always have a flight simulator duel with a new team member to assess their flying ability, and Marlise was the first one to ever..."

Asante lifted a hand to stop me. "Yes, but what does she look like? Can you show me an image?"

I tapped at the lookup on my left sleeve, and projected a holo image in midair above the table. "This is Marlise standing next to her fighter. The dead thing on the ground is..."

"The dead thing on the ground is messy and irrelevant." Asante studied the holo for a moment then nodded. "Marlise isn't beautiful."

I glared at him. "Yes, she is."

"No, she isn't. We can ask everyone in the MeetUp to vote on the question if you like, they're all nosily staring at your holo, but they'll all say the same. Marlise is just a moderately attractive girl."

I shut down the holo. "Her looks don't matter. I didn't fall in love with them, I fell in love with her adventurous soul, and the way she..."

Asante raised his imperious hand again. "But her looks do matter. Given you're so handsome, the fact she isn't beautiful is the key to your relationship dynamics. I suspect Marlise finds you as irresistible as everyone else, and that influenced her decision to split up with her boyfriend."

I frowned. "You're saying I ruined things for Marlise exactly the same way that I ruined things for Gemelle?"

"I'm not saying that at all," said Asante. "You tricked Gemelle into splitting up with a boyfriend that she cared for, but your Marlise made a free choice to end a relationship she didn't want. That's entirely different."

I hoped he was right.

"If you have anything like the same eager, dumb-struck expression on your face when you talk to Marlise as when you talk about her," continued Asante, "then the girl should have realized you're in love with her. If you aren't getting any response from her, then I think it's because of her own lack of confidence. She can't believe you could be seriously interested in someone who isn't beautiful. You're scared to propose to her without an indication that she's interested, and she's scared to give you that indication because she thinks it will embarrass you and make her look a fool."

"So what do I do? Propose again?"

"No," said Asante. "If you want marriage rather than a quick tumble, then you don't just need to convince your Marlise that you're interested in her, but that you'll stay interested in her when other people keep throwing themselves at you in the future. You have to build a proper foundation before you propose again. Talk to Marlise and tell her what you said to me earlier. Say that she's very important to you as both a deputy and a friend. Do you think you can say that coherently?"

"I hope I can, but she's on a different planet at the moment."

Asante gave me a pitying look. "You have a perfectly functioning lookup, Drago. You can use it to call the girl."

I realized he was right. A proposal had to be made in person, but I could call Marlise to tell her she was important to me. I started mentally planning the conversation. Could I start by saying I was calling to check she'd arrived safely? It was preposterous to call a Military officer to check she'd managed to safely walk through a few interstellar portals, but...

My lookup chose that moment to start chiming.

"Chaos take it!" said Asante in despairing tones. "I hate those things disturbing the ambiance of my MeetUp. Have you been away so long that you've forgotten I insist on people keeping their lookups set to only receive emergency calls?"

"My lookup *is* in emergency mode!" I stood up and stared down at the call information on my lookup. General Hiraga was calling me and that meant...

I bit my lip and stabbed a finger at my lookup to take the call. "Yes, sir."

"Sorry to disturb you when you're on leave, Major Tell Dramis, but I need to discuss a possible future posting with you." General Hiraga paused. "I see you're not alone. This matter is highly confidential, so I'll put this call on hold until you find a suitably private location."

Her image froze on the screen. I kept staring at it for a few seconds longer, then sagged back down into my chair, letting myself flop across the table so my head rested on my arms.

"Are you all right, Drago?" asked Asante.

I needed a moment longer to get myself under control before I could risk lifting my head. I discovered everyone in the MeetUp was staring at me.

"I'm sorry I acted a little oddly then, but when you get a personal emergency call from a General..." I had to break off for a moment because my voice was shaking. "Well, it usually means someone very close to you has been killed."

Asante patted me on the shoulder. "That's all right, Drago."

I rubbed a hand across my forehead. "I don't understand why General Hiraga scared me to death by calling me directly herself, instead of getting Command Support to put through the call. I'd better go and see what she wants."

I headed out of the MeetUp to a square paved area with a huge central laser light sculpture. The square was surrounded by eating places and entertainment venues, so there were plenty of people wandering to and fro, while others sat on benches admiring the dazzling light strands of the sculpture that lit up the night sky. I needed somewhere far more private than this.

There were half a dozen portals scattered round the square. I headed for the nearest one, pausing to think when I reached it. If I portalled home to my clan hall, then I'd probably meet a dozen members of the clan on my way to my room. They'd all stop to either welcome me home because they hadn't seen me since my return, or ask why I was back so early from my evening out. Where did I know that would be totally deserted after dark?

I finally remembered the place where my clan went to celebrate the birthday of our clan founder, checked the code on my lookup, and dialled the portal. As soon as it established, I stepped through to a beach that was lit only by the stars and the twin moons of Zeus, and walked across to the familiar statue made of glittering diamene.

It was too dark to read the neat inscription about how a boy of 17 had tragically drowned on this beach, but my hand could trace the outline of the larger letters below that had been carved roughly by hand with a laser pen, and I knew exactly what they said. "Of course I didn't drown, you idiots. I can swim like a fish!"

I saluted the statue, took a last look round to check the beach was empty, and could see no sign of life except for the shadowy shape of a nocturnal Zeus hawk swooping low above me. I tapped my lookup to reactivate General Hiraga's call. "I'm now totally alone on a beach, sir."

"Excellent," said General Hiraga. "I'm talking to you on a secure link, Major Tell Dramis, because this information is being strictly restricted to key personnel. We don't want the news channels getting hold of it before the official announcement."

I blinked. That explained why she'd made this call herself, instead of getting Command Support to make it for her, but why would my future posting interest the newzies?

"Humanity founded far too many colony worlds far too fast during Exodus century," said General Hiraga. "The strain of that reckless overexpansion led to the near total collapse of civilization, a situation that must not be repeated, so now expansion proceeds at a carefully judged, sustainable pace. For the colonization of Delta sector, the Military were set the target of opening about two hundred worlds to match the number in each of the existing sectors, at a rate of two worlds a year."

I'd no idea why I was being given a history lesson, but I daren't interrupt the formidable General Hiraga to ask questions. The most terrifying creatures humanity had ever encountered were the chimera of Thetis, but in my opinion General Hiraga was a close second when she lost her temper.

"That meant it took a century for the colonization of Delta sector to be completed," continued General Hiraga. "When the Planet First teams moved on from Delta sector to Epsilon sector, it was decided that the number of worlds opening for colonization each year should increase from two to three. That rate of expansion is now being maintained as we colonize Kappa sector."

She paused. "The final Kappa sector worlds should open for colonization in about forty years from now. We'll need Planet First operations to be well advanced in the next sector, Zeta, by then. Since the stellar survey and selection of prospective colony worlds in Zeta sector will take decades, the General Marshal and representatives of Joint Sector High Congress Committee have authorized work to begin on the initial stellar survey of Zeta sector at the beginning of next year."

Chaos, now I understood why the newzies would be interested. The merest hint that the Military were starting work in Zeta sector would have every newzie channel screaming in excitement about a new sector for humanity.

General Hiraga gave me a thin-lipped smile. "The current portal relay network will have to be extended into the heart of Zeta sector, to allow Planet First Stellar Survey to set up their base there. When the Military first extended the portal relay network into Kappa sector, the news channels were told about it in advance, and reported every unexpected difficulty and delay. We don't want that happening again, so this time there'll be no official announcement until the Stellar Survey base is actually operational."

By now I'd worked out what she must be going to say next, what assignment I was going to be offered. I had an odd breathless moment.

"We need a fighter team to go into Zeta sector and set up those portal relays, Major," said General Hiraga. "You have a very experienced team, glowing recommendations from your last commanding officer, and a reputation for responding rapidly and effectively to unexpected dangers. I realize your team has only just completed a long and arduous Planet First assignment, but there's time for you all to have two months of leave before you head into Zeta sector."

Her voice took on a heavily formal note. "Major Tell Dramis, I must warn you that this assignment will involve using drop portals to reach uncharted star systems that may contain extreme hazards. You are under no pressure to volunteer for this mission, and you may take a reasonable amount of time to consider your decision."

I didn't need time to consider this. There'd obviously be risks portalling into the total unknown, but I couldn't turn down a chance like this. "I wish to volunteer, sir. Should I start contacting my team immediately?"

General Hiraga nodded. "We'll want to know which of them are volunteering as soon as possible, so we have plenty of time to select any necessary substitutes. You must make sure they understand the need for absolute secrecy, Major, and formally warn them of the potential danger involved before asking if they wish to volunteer."

"Yes, sir. Thank you, sir."

She ended the call, and I took a deep breath. This wasn't exactly the conversation I'd been thinking of having with Marlise, but...

I tapped at my lookup, setting up a secure call to Marlise, and waited for about thirty seconds before the call was accepted with sound only. "I don't know what time it is on Zeus," said a resigned voice, "but I'd like to point out it's three o'clock in the morning here."

"Sorry, Marlise, I totally forgot to check time zones, but I'd have had to call you anyway. I've just been contacted by General Hiraga."

She groaned. "What did you do this time?"

"Nothing! She wanted to discuss our next assignment."

"Already? We've only been on leave for a day."

"The assignment doesn't start for another two months," I said.

"If it doesn't start for two months, why did you have to call me at three o'clock in the morning?"

"Because General Hiraga wants to know which of my team are willing to volunteer for this."

"Volunteer?" The call suddenly changed to include vision. Marlise was sitting up in bed, wearing a sadly respectable sleep suit. "This sounds interesting."

I grinned. "Captain Weldon, you are being told this information in strictest confidence."

She gave a brisk nod. "Noted, sir."

"I'm speaking to you on a secure link. Are you totally alone?"

She lifted her pillow, theatrically looked underneath it, and put it down again. "I'm totally alone, sir. Where are they sending us?"

My grin widened. "Zeta sector."

"What! Why?"

"To start setting up the portal relay network there. Our team has the chance to be the first human beings to enter Zeta sector!"

Marlise grinned back at me. "I volunteer, sir."

"You know you can't volunteer before I give you the formal warning."

"So get on with it!"

I sighed. "Captain Weldon, I must formally warn you that the assignment will involve using drop portals to reach uncharted star systems that may contain extreme hazards. You are under no pressure to volunteer for this mission."

"I formally volunteer, sir." She shook her head. "I can't believe this is really happening. Drago, if you're making this up to tease me..."

"I wouldn't do that," I said. "I'd hate to upset you, Marlise. You're very important to me, as both a deputy and a friend."

She looked oddly startled. "Thank you." She seemed about to say something else, but changed her mind, so there was a moment of silence. "I'd better let you carry on and call the rest of the team now," she said at last.

I reluctantly shut down the secure link, frowned at the blank screen of my lookup, and thought through Marlise's reaction just then. She usually acted the part of a long-suffering friend, who was tolerating my follies out of resigned loyalty, but I'd caught a glimpse of something deeper and far more vulnerable. I wasn't deluding myself into thinking Marlise thought me irresistible, but there was something more than just friendship there.

If Marlise cared for me even a fraction as much as I cared for her, then I had every chance of making things work between us. I'd wrecked things for me and Gemelle out of childish selfishness, but I was definitely older now, hopefully wiser, and I had Asante to advise me as well. After running a MeetUp for two decades, Asante was an expert on relationships.

Things would be different this time. I knew Marlise was perfect for me, and I was willing to do anything I could to be perfect for her. We'd soon be exploring new physical territory together in Zeta sector. I hoped we'd be exploring new emotional territory together as well. I hoped we'd be exploring new challenges together for the rest of our lives.

APPENDIX – INFORMATION FOR INTERSTELLAR TRAVELLERS

EARTH

Original home world of humanity.
During Exodus century (2310-2409) most of the population of Earth left for new worlds that were less polluted and overcrowded.
Physically located in the centre of Alpha sector, Earth is administered by the main board of Hospital Earth under the moderate culture of Gamma sector.

Warning notes for travellers:-
Hospital Earth requests all visitors to avoid using the "ape" word to refer to its wards.

Special travel information:-
Earth is the only world with more than one inhabited continent. Visitors wishing to travel between continents need to use the inter-continental portals at Transit facilities.

Special safety information:-
Hospital Earth allows its wards free access to all public areas on Earth. Medical experts advise that there is no health risk to visiting Earth or interacting with the wards of Hospital Earth, however some visitors prefer to take the safety precaution of only consuming food and drink from sealed cartons in private.
Earth has extensive ruined cities and wilderness areas that contain dangerous animals and lingering pollution hazards. Visitors leaving the designated safe zones do so entirely at their own risk.

Earth is the only inhabited world that suffers from regular solar storms. These affect the portal network, causing portal shutdowns that can last for periods of up to three days. Visitors are strongly advised to pay close attention to any solar storm warnings

Hospital Earth accepts no liability for any injuries or inconvenience caused to visitors. The main board of Hospital Earth wishes all visitors to Earth a pleasant stay.

ALPHA SECTOR

201 Inhabited Star Systems
1610 Representatives in Parliament of Planets
Colonization began in 2310
Capital planet Adonis

Warning notes for travellers:-
The worlds of Alpha sector are noted for their wealth and historic buildings. They have widely varying customs since many of them were colonized directly from specific areas of Earth. Visitors are strongly advised to check the detailed cultural information for each world before visiting it. They should also be aware that some worlds were selected for colonization when the Planet First selection criteria were less stringent. Length of day, and some other physical conditions, may be slightly outside the current norms.

Special safety information:-
During the partial collapse of civilization after Exodus century, the population of Cassandra was forced to move continent. The sunshine intensity on the new inhabited continent of Cassandra is considered to be a low level health hazard. Travellers are warned to obtain individual medical advice before visiting the planet Cassandra.

BETA SECTOR

203 Inhabited Star Systems
1431 Representatives in Parliament of Planets
Colonization began in 2370
Capital planet Zeus

Warning notes for travellers:-
Beta sector has a distinctive clan based culture, and is widely regarded as the most permissive of all the sectors. Around 17% of marriages in Beta sector involve triad rather than duo relationships. Betans have a minimal nudity taboo, and you will hear words in common usage that are regarded as unacceptable in other sectors.

GAMMA SECTOR

203 Inhabited Star Systems
826 Representatives in Parliament of Planets
First stage colonization began in 2381
Capital planet Asgard

Warning notes for travellers:-
Colonization of Gamma sector began in 2381, but the partial collapse of civilization after Exodus century, and the Thetis crisis, meant the final Gamma sector worlds weren't opened until over two centuries later. The older Gamma sector worlds are fiercely proud of their struggle for survival during two centuries of chaos.

Gamma sector is widely regarded as having moderate values, and despite its small population has very strong political influence. The votes of its planetary representatives are often the deciding factor in issues that divide the much larger Alpha and Beta sectors. Any assumption of superiority by visitors from Alphan or Betan planets may be met with hostility.

DELTA SECTOR

202 Inhabited Star Systems
429 Representatives in Parliament of Planets
Colonization began in 2600
Capital planet Isis

Warning notes for travellers:-
Delta sector has very conservative views on the level of intimacy appropriate before marriage. Public displays of affection, such as kissing and holding hands, are strongly discouraged and can lead to prosecution under the decency laws.

EPSILON SECTOR

201 Inhabited Star Systems
201 Representatives in Parliament of Planets
Colonization began in 2698
Capital planet still undetermined

Warning notes for travellers:-
Epsilon sector is still in the frontier stage of colonization, and most settlements are small farming communities. You should be prepared for basic living conditions and the lack of many public amenities. Due to the fact more male than female colonists arrive on the frontier, triad marriages of one woman and two men are strongly encouraged.

Additional notes from the Epsilon Colonization Advisory Service:-
If you're visiting the frontier worlds of Epsilon, why not consider changing that visit into a lifetime commitment to a new world? The worlds of Epsilon actively welcome colonists of all types, but especially women, as well as those with qualifications in teaching and all areas of medicine. Contact the Epsilon Colonization Advisory Service for more information on how you can help build the future!

KAPPA SECTOR

The worlds of Kappa sector are mostly still in either Planet First or Colony Ten phase. Those worlds open for full colonization are running under standard Colony Ten law. Prospective colonists should contact the Kappa Colonization Advisory Service for more information.

Warning notes for travellers:-
Travel to Kappa sector worlds is strictly limited to incoming colonists.

ZETA SECTOR

Uncharted space.

Additional historical note:-
Zeta sector was originally scheduled to be colonized after Epsilon sector, but Beta sector's period of independence as the Second Roman Empire resulted in Planet First efforts being redirected to Kappa sector.

Message From Janet Edwards

Thank you for reading Earth 2788. Since I first wrote this collection, two of the shorter stories have become the inspiration for much longer novellas. The story about Jarra has been continued to be Earth and Fire, and the story about Amalie has been continued to become Frontier.

Please visit my website, www.janetedwards.com, to see the current list of my books. You can also make sure you don't miss future books by signing up to get an email alert when there's a new release

Best wishes from Janet Edwards

Made in the USA
Columbia, SC
12 August 2017